Love to Hurt You

Love to Hurt You

Rahul Saini

JUGGERNAUT BOOKS
KS House, 118 Shahpur Jat, New Delhi 110049, India

First published by Juggernaut Books 2019

10 9 8 7 6 5 4 3 2 1

This is a work of fiction. Any resemblance to persons, living or dead, or to actual incidents is purely coincidental.

P-ISBN: 978-93-5345-067-0
E-ISBN: 978-93-5345-069-4

Typeset in Adobe Caslon Pro by R. Ajith Kumar, Noida

Printed and bound at Thomson Press India Ltd

Preface

Why do we read stories? And why do we write stories? A tearjerker, an edge-of-the-seat thriller, a rib-tickling comedy or any other 'successful' story, what do they all have in common? They ride our emotions. If stories can't manage that, there is something missing in them.

It took me five years to write this book, along with another one, because my intention was to break away from the template I had been following for my previous books. The idea was to make the reader sink into the minds of the characters, love or hate them for who they are. A simple psychological exploration of them.

I must point out that unlike my earlier books, this one is not suitable for younger readers because of graphic content in terms of sex and violence.

This is an age governed by the principle 'bad is the new good'. The motive of this book is to highlight the reality of the times we are living in.

Writing this book has been an exciting journey for me and I hope you will enjoy it as much as I did.

'Let us consider an ugly soul, intemperate and unjust . . . full of a great number of desires and the most profound anxieties.'

Plotinus, *The Enneads*

Part 1

The pursuit of fulfilment

1

Sasha

The woman who has men wrapped around her fingers

She always wore eight solitaires – one on each finger, each one worth five million. It was her way of showing the world that she had the power and the money to have men wrapped around her fingers.

She was done with her routine now. She was done putting the man through the most excruciating pain he had ever experienced. His balls were swollen red to the size of a hen's eggs. His torso was marked with the fresh, throbbing lashes from the whipping he had just received. The whip had struck remarkably hard at one particular spot – right below his left nipple. It had ripped a good inch of flesh off his chest.

Sasha looks at the man, his limbs tied to the four posts of the bed. She tilts her head and observes him like a cat sizing up its prey. Neither of them has a shred of clothing on. The man lies spreadeagled on the bed, the few things touching his bare skin are the red satin bed sheet under him, the ropes tying his limbs to the bedposts, and the piece of cloth that gags him. Sasha draws closer, swinging her leg over him so that the man is now between her legs. She sits on his belly and looks into his eyes. She sees pain, she sees fear, she sees a desperate urge to get out of her grip and run away. She smiles. She caresses the red wound on the man's chest. Blood is oozing out of it – a bright red drop swelling, shining. She keeps staring at it till the drop grows larger. Failing to hold its round boundary, it slides down leaving a thin red line along the side of the man's chest, soaking into the red satin bed sheet, leaving a dark stain much bigger than its own size. Sasha traces that thin red line with her finger up to the point where the skin had come off and presses on it hard. The man can't scream out in pain because of his gag. His body just shakes and trembles. The tip of her finger is red from his blood. She sticks out her tongue and slowly licks the man's blood off her finger. She smiles again. 'It's funny, isn't it? Everything that comes out of a man's body is salty.'

The man does not reply. He just gapes at Sasha, wide-eyed with panic and fear.

Putting both her hands on the man's chest, Sasha looks at him again, drawing pleasure from his pain. Her long manicured fingers with long, bright red nails glow like jewels when they dig into his skin as she swings her leg off the man, leaves the bed and walks over to the window to gaze at the cityscape.

In her late forties, Sasha's slender, naked figure deceptively suggests a much younger age. Her skin is smooth and flawless and her breasts round and firm, symmetrically decorated with big, dark nipples. She pulls on a thin chiffon robe which does nothing to hide her form but only outlines her figure like a ghostly mist.

'You were not as brave as you said you would be,' she says looking down at him as she walks towards him, 'when you met me at the bar downstairs. How strong you sounded then.' She shakes her head. '"I have made women scream louder than they knew they were capable of," you said. And look at you now.' Untying the rope around one of his ankles, she continues, 'I wish men were smarter.' She frees his other ankle. 'I wish they knew how delicate and fragile they are, how vulnerable, how weak in front of money, how they agree to do anything for it.' She moves on to the ropes around his wrists.

After the man's limbs are free she removes the gag from his mouth. He is panting heavily as he rubs his wrist to sooth the sting of the rope that had held him tight till just a few seconds ago.

'Would you like to have some water?' Sasha asks.

The man nods.

She pours him a glass of water. The water sparkles in the dim light of the room like a glass full of diamonds. The man empties the glass in a single gulp.

'Amazing, isn't it? We never understand the value of anything until we are deprived of it. Water. We humans are foolish like that, aren't we? It's almost evil, some would say, from the viewpoint of the things we are insensitive to.'

The man has lost interest in what Sasha is saying. He just wants to leave. He gets up, his balls still sore. He is not able to stand erect due to the pain. He starts gathering the clothes he had so excitedly taken off earlier and flung all over the room. Little did he know then what awaited him.

His disinterest in her words pisses Sasha off. She goes up to him and holds him by his arm as he is bending to retrieve his pants from the floor. 'I would pay you twenty thousand more if you would step out into the hallway nude, walk to the stairs and then put these clothes on.'

The man jerks his arm out of her grip.

'Fifty thousand more.'

The man shoots her a heated glance, clutching harder on to his clothes which he has in his hands now.

'One lakh more,' she says.

The man stands there, still glaring at her. She smiles,

turns around and takes out a thick bundle of notes from the locker.

The man drops his clothes to the floor.

Sasha walks to the man and stands in front of him. Then she grabs him by his balls as he lets out a little squeak. 'You know this money, she is a goddess who grabs all men by their balls. And she can make them do *anything*.'

The man opens the door of the hotel room and walks to the stairs without a single piece of clothing on. All his clothes are rolled up into a messy ball in his hands. He stands on the first step of the staircase and puts on his clothes. He turns around and looks at Sasha who is standing in the doorway of the room, wearing the same thin chiffon robe which is as transparent as the thin morning mist. She smiles at the man and beckons him with one of her diamond-laden fingers. He obeys her like a dog.

'Take this money–' She gives him the wad of notes and then grabs the collar of his shirt and looks at him with wild, animal eyes. She pulls him to herself and indulges in a long, passionate kiss and then withdraws – 'and never show me your face again,' she says.

She shuts the door and walks to the sofa next to the huge window that runs from the floor to the ceiling. She is in the luxury suite on the eleventh floor of a grand seven-star hotel. She picks up the cigar lying on the table next to her and chews on its bud as she looks out of the window at the cityscape again. Streams of light are flowing on the roads as little shining beads of hot gold. The tall buildings dotted with lights look like toys from the distance. All these lights, all these rooms and all the men inside them – she could control them all. She could control any potent man on earth, as long as his hot blood pumped and harden his dick at the sight and touch of her beautiful, enticing body. This gives her immense satisfaction, the feeling of sweet revenge against her husband and every man who has been unfaithful.

2

Maya

Who ends one's life if it is worth keeping

It's a strange feeling to write down your last words. It's stress coupled with a kind of relaxation. It is like dying slowly with complete consciousness, knowing that your life is moving closer to its end with every word you put down. Tomorrow I shall be no more.

No one ever ends their life if it is worth keeping. I have lost all reason and will to live. I have forced myself to live for a long time. It kills me to see how my sadness saddens my mother. She keeps a check on me 24/7 and my misery makes her miserable. I go days without taking a shower, I skip meals, I stay in my bed till two in the afternoon. When I am no longer around, she will forget me and be happy and cheerful like she was before.

Arun, why did you have to die? Why did you leave me alone? We had made a promise. You said we would be together forever. And you left me. I don't know how to live without you. I don't *want* to live without you. The vanilla ice cream with mangoes has lost its taste, something that we used to enjoy together, something that used to excite us and make us fight for the last bite. The other day Mom got me a bowl full of it. I didn't even have the desire to taste it. It reminded me of our evenings in your apartment on the seventh floor. You would cut the mangoes and I would take the ice cream out, tearing off the soggy, sticky packing.

They say death is nothing but a barrier that is to be crossed by the soul from one life to another. You crossed this barrier last year. You must have found life again somewhere in this world. Let me cross this barrier now. And then, let me find you so that we can be together. I am so haunted by your memories, by your absence that only death can be my escape from this cruelty.

It was a drug overdose, the doctors said. Why was I not there at the party? If I had been there, I would have stopped you. You would still be alive. I still feel it's my fault. I am guilty, I am the culprit. I have no right to live.

I stare at the empty bottle of sleeping pills on the table in front of me. I am already drowsy. It's only a matter of minutes before I sleep, never to wake up again. I get up from my chair and take in my room. I have grown up here. I look at the framed picture of Arun on my study table. His broad smile and optimistic eyes shining brightly. I pick it up and lie on the bed, resting my head on the pillow. It's a silent night. Someone is parking their car after a long day at work. His daughter is singing happily 'Papa ghar aa gaye!' I stare at the still ceiling fan for a while. I hold Arun's picture tight against my chest and I close my eyes. I am taking one last moment of our togetherness with me as I pass on.

Tomorrow morning there will be no me. Or maybe I will live on in someone else's memory. And my memory will have a lot to say – a long, sad tale. Maybe that is how I will live even after I die. Maybe that's how all dead people live on. Maybe people never really die. Everyone is immortal.

3

Garun

Living the golden dream

They say everyone is entitled to one true love in life. My true love is money and fame.

Another day has come to an end. Are things to settle peacefully to sleep or are things waiting to kick into some good action for the night? The elevator is ascending to the penthouse on the twenty-fifth floor of the most coveted residential tower in the city. The building is a landmark. It is a dream residence for many. The form of the building itself speaks of power and glamour. The fantastic building has a pentagonal base with five triangular glass petals tinted golden copper running up to a mighty height of one hundred and fifteen metres, tilting slightly outwards like the petals of a flower that is about to bloom. The glass facade encases the tall pentagonal pyramid form of the building that housed seventy-five luxury apartments. Garun reaches the top of this copper-golden, transparent flower and turns the key to his penthouse. The rich and famous live here. In fact, to be rich and famous is a prerequisite to own a flat here. Film stars, cricketers, supermodels, politicians – everyone residing in this building is someone important. And right now, Garun stands above them all. This is the gift he had demanded from his parents before they moved to London a year ago.

'I have to go. It's the best opportunity I could have been offered,' his father had told him.

'I don't want you to go, Dad!' Garun had pretended. He knew he had to dig his way through to get what he wanted.

'We have to go, Garun. Please try to understand,' his mother had said.

'What! You are going with him? What am I supposed to do? Live here alone?' he had exclaimed.

'We will make sure you can come and live with us after some time. It's just a matter of a few years. By the time you finish college, things would have settled,' his mother had explained, giving him a hug.

Garun had put on a long face. He had to keep the act going.

'Okay, tell us how we can make up for it,' his mother had offered.

He had hesitated for a moment. He didn't want to wreck his chance.

'I don't know . . . how can anything make up for you guys not being here.'

'Come on. There must be something that you want . . . something that would make you happy?'

Garun pushes open the door to his penthouse and throws the keys on the side table in the foyer. He is tired. He goes and stands by the huge living room window. The city is buzzing, speckled with lights from the nightclubs where people are partying hard, drinking, smoking and dancing, with their arms around other people's bodies, feeling them, getting high on the pleasure. The cars streaking down the roads look like streams of glowing lava. Peering down at the city below him, he smiles. He has big dreams, as big and bright as this huge city. And he knows he will achieve them all. For he has always achieved everything he has wanted in the past, by hook or by crook.

When his parents had insisted on giving him a parting gift, he had put forth his demand – an apartment in the Golden Lotus. It was the address of the rich and the famous. It was an address he wanted to flaunt to the world. At first his dad was shocked. 'The apartments there are bloody expensive!' he had exclaimed. But his mother had convinced him soon enough. 'I want to see him happy before we leave,' she had said. 'Come on! I know we can afford it. And buying property never hurts. What have we ever done for our kid?

I know it's very important to earn money because that's the only way we can give our child a happy and secure future and we must grab the opportunity you have been offered. If this makes him happy then why can't we do this for him? The price of that apartment is only going to rise. When he joins us in London we will sell it off.' Not only had she prevailed, she had also coaxed his father into buying a penthouse instead of a simple apartment.

When his parents had left, Garun was happy as a one-year-old baby being tickled in the belly. He was free. He could do whatever he wanted. He did not have to sneak out of the house to smoke. He did not have to hide his tobacco breath with mouth freshener and chewing gum. He could watch porn on the fifty-two-inch LED TV without fear, without muting the volume. He could wank off right there. He could enjoy himself without any restrictions.

Now his fridge is always full of beer and meat.

He opens the fridge and peeps inside. He is thirsty but how much can one drink at home, alone? He goes into the living room and flips through his DVD collection. Nothing exciting. How much porn can one watch. How much can one fap looking at the dumb blondes on the TV screen. Where's the fun in that. He can't slap their ass. He can't even squeeze their tits. No, there is no satisfaction in simply cumming like that. He wants some real action. He has to go out. He has to find a girl to sleep with tonight.

4

Maya

Advice from a stranger

The white sterile space and the electronic beeps first made me think that I was in some kind of an afterlife transitional tunnel. The light was blinding. It took me a few seconds to realize that the blue cloud floating around me was a nurse on duty. Someone had saved me. It must have been my mother.

The nurse notices that I am conscious. She smiles at me and says, 'Good morning.'

I am confused. I nod my head and fake a smile.

'You must hate this world an awful lot. A whole lot of mess came out of you when we pumped your stomach. A whole bottle of pills you must have gulped down.'

My eyes well up. Tears run down my cheeks uncontrollably.

'Hey, hey, come on.' She rushes towards me and embraces me with warm affection. 'It's going to be okay, trust me, the worst is over.'

'Who brought me here?' I struggle to speak through my sobs.

'Your mother. And like every mother, she loves you more than she loves herself.'

I have always been a reason for her troubles. 'Is she . . . is she here? Is she in the hospital?'

'Yes, my dear, she is very much here. But we don't let people into the ICU all day. Only during visiting hours. If you have reached the ICU it means you need some peace and rest.' She smiles. 'But if you want, we can ask her to come in.'

'No, not right now.' The words fly out of my mouth like a reflex.

'It's okay,' the nurse responds.' If you need anything at all, let me know. You just have to press this button.' She points to the little blue button by my bed.

'Thank you.' I nod.

'Now you take rest.'

I close my eyes and nod again.

The room goes quiet but I can still sense the nurse's presence. After a few seconds I hear her voice. 'Can I please be your friend? Not only a nurse?'

I look at her. She takes my silence as a yes.

'Just a little friendly advice – nothing is as bad for which one should give up one's life.' She waits by the door for a few moments and then leaves. Long after she is gone, her words keep echoing in my mind – *nothing is as bad for which one should give up one's life*. But for some reason, her words don't have any effect on me. All I can think of is my mother. Her horror and panic when she would have found me in a semi-dead state. How she would have screamed and wept hugging me tight to her chest. How she would have fumbled through her phonebook with shaking hands to find the hospital number. She can never manage to find the number of any of her friends on the phone in the first go. She always dials a wrong number and then ends up talking to that 'wrong person' for hours. How she would have held her hands together and prayed for my life continuously till the ambulance would have arrived.

She should not have saved me, she should have let me die. Her whole life revolves around me. With me not there any more, she would have learned to live for herself – live the life she deserves. Why do parents devote their whole life to their children? Why do they stop living for themselves the minute their child is born? Why do they love them so much? She loves me more than anyone can ever love me. I was wrong in thinking that she would find happiness if I go away. Was I able to find my happiness with Arun not there any more? The void that a loved one leaves can never be filled. It stays forever like an aching gap in your heart, killing a part of you each time that void comes to life with the memory of the departed. It was very selfish of me to put my mother through all this pain. Of all the people left in my life, she is the one I love the most. I want to see her. I want to see her now!

5

Garun

His kind of wonderland

Fine on plucking flowers: Rs 1000.

This is the first thing I notice as I enter the gate of the college. It's my first day. I don't really need any degree or to attend any college. I am quite good at dealing with people and earning money. But I live in a shitty society where no one would take me seriously if I don't have a few degrees to throw in their faces. So – my presence here.

It's a lavish campus. The building looks ancient. Must be a hundred years old at least. Has the same stupid arches and columns we see all around in CP. I cross the pavements, gardens and the corridors and it looks like a different world I have stepped into. *And I like it*! I haven't seen such a free environment in real life before and never could have imagined it in a school or college. There are couples kissing, hugging, holding hands, fingers interlocked. Some have beer cans in their hands, some are smoking. Most of them look like rebels who people would shun as outcasts. This place just rocks!

It's eleven fifteen and I am fifteen minutes late for my class but I don't think it makes any difference. It's gonna be a lame-ass class delivered by a lame-ass teacher who would not know even the tiniest shit about the subject he will come to teach. I enter the classroom and am comforted by what I see. There is no teacher there. Many couples are sitting together. Some are looking into each other's eyes. The girls are smiling shyly. The guys want to hold them and kiss them, on the mouth. I need to get a girl to keep me entertained in class soon. There is no greater joy in life than to have a girl sit next to you who lets you run your hand up her skirt, as a lame-ass loser teacher rambles on about something that you don't even give the thinnest fuck about.

Seems like the teacher is gonna take some time to come. Till then I should not disturb these people as they shove their tongues down each other's throats. I should go find a place to sit.

I take a quick look around and I see the girls in the class are hot! Tight low-waist jeans and tight tops. Some of them are wearing tight buttoned-down shirts with the top three buttons open. It's not only revealing the cleavage but also giving a good view of their bra. There are a few girls in tight hot pants and loose T-shirts. One has a pierced eyebrow. Most of them have cup sizes that you imagine or look at in the bathroom at night before you toot your horn and go off to sleep. But I don't want to approach any of them right now. That would just label me as the 'desperate dude' who only wants to lick their tits and give them his meat injections. I need to be a part of a group first. A 'cool group'. The one that everyone worships, the one that sets the trends, the one that tells everyone which class to attend and which not to.

There is a group of boys I see sitting next to the window at the end of the classroom. They look cool, all four of them. Two of them are sitting on the ledge and the other two have their chairs turned so that their backs are towards the rest of the room. They seem to be regular members at the gym – it is clear from their biceps and shoulders. Cool haircuts. Tight T-shirts that highlight their build. The in crowd! I want to gel with them.

'She is the real deal, man!' one of them says with a badass smile as he looks at the rest. 'And last night she was just awesome! We went to a bar first. A couple of drinks. Then we just drove around. Half an hour or so. She kept laughing. Was so high. Kept touching my junk and giggling. It gave me such a hard-on, man! It was so tough to control myself that time! I kept gripping the steering wheel so hard I could almost feel it squeezing thin in my hands. I just wanted to get on with some humping. So I took her to the Highland Hotel. And there *we did it*!'

'Cool, man!' The other two gave him a high five. It is only then that they realize that I am standing next to them. Listening.

'Garun.' I extend my hand forward with a warm smile of appreciation for his achievement to the guy who was talking.

'Tarush,' said the guy who got his dick sucked last night.

Quick handshakes with the rest of the guys as they all tell me their names. But who the fuck cares what their names are anyway. I am never going to remember them.

'First day?' Tarush asks.

'Yeah bro!'

'And by the way, before I forget,' the cultural committee had a meeting in the morning and I have been elected president,' Tarush says, nodding his head and looking at everyone and smiling as if he has become the prime minister of the country. 'So if any of you wants to show any of your *special talents* during the talent hunt, let me know. I will put you on stage.'

'Cool!' I say. 'I can sing.'

Everyone bursts out laughing. 'Okay, so you are a *poop star* already?'

These dickheads are more stupid than I thought but I don't react. I just stand there quietly and an awkward silence prevails for a bit.

Just then I see someone enter the class and I really can't believe my eyes. It's Maya – the girl who made history with her debut novel last year. The one who won that award and shit. The bitch I hate so much.

'Drooling already?' Tarush gives me a nudge with a devilish smile as I snap out of my thoughts.

'I know, man! Just look at her tits! De-li-ci-ous!' the guy sitting next to Tarush says.

'What is she doing here?' I am actually confused.

'Some serious shit, man! She was one of those *bright students*. The ones that look down upon the likes of us like worms and insects. Got hooked up with a dude from fine arts. He was a hard-ass junkie. Died of an overdose. Some say he died in a car crash but I think that's only a pathetic, sorry story some of his friends made up to save the goody goody image that he had so successfully planted in people's minds. He was a true con artist, man. Anyway, after he died, she went into some depression and shit. Stopped attending college and wrote a novel. I don't read but people who have read it say it is pure fuck. Total waste of time. But it went on to . . .'

'I know that story. But what is she doing here? In first year?'

'Fell short of attendance. Had to repeat the year.'

So the lady luck is licking my balls today. Couldn't have asked for more! I just need to pocket this girl. She is my passport to success and fame!

6

Maya

A strange, familiar voice

I want to scream! I want to shout my throat to shreds. Why is life so cruel? Why does it whip and lash our gentle, naked soul bloody? What have I done to deserve this living hell of agony? Everyone tells me to be *brave*. But no one understands that although they see me alive, I am dead.

In the stillness of the night, Maya can hear her own heartbeat. She can hear her own breath.

'It's okay, just stick in there. You are gonna be fine,' she hears a voice say, almost a faint, light whisper. She looks around the room confused – there is no one there.

'You have a very long life ahead of you,' the voice continues, 'proof of which is that you are still alive, after trying so hard to kill yourself.'

She stands still in the room. Only the night lamp kept on the study table is lit but her eyes are well adjusted to the light. She can see everything clearly. All the framed pictures on the wall, her bed, the bed sheets with quotes from Rumi printed with floral motives around them. Her pillow in the plain white pillow cover lined with a broad white, delicate floral lace. There is no one else in the room. Who is speaking? Who is there? She stands there staring into the space. Silent. A thin line floats in front of her eyes. A strand of hair? Waving and twirling in the air, it gently settles on her pillow.

'But you have to move on,' comes the voice again. It is coming from that thin line, that strand of hair, which now moves, vibrates and distorts as the voice speaks. 'Just look around this room. You have clutched on to my memories so hard. You are not letting go.'

Maya looks at the almirah set against the wall. It is full of the gifts Arun had given her. The chair next to it is piled with the T-shirts he had given her. It was a ritual of sorts for them – they would gift each other a T-shirt once every month with a special thought printed on it, many times with a picture of both of them together. There is also a whole bunch of other things like keychains, soft toys, cute photo frames, etc. She opens the almirah and stares at the gifts blankly. She is transported back to the past. She remembers the time when Arun had proposed to her. They were in fifth standard back then. It seemed like a joke. That time they were only good friends who would share all their secrets with each other; tell each other every detail of what was going on in their lives and take suggestions from each other. They would take turns to do each other's homework. They had cried together when Arun's dog, Ruffle, had died. They were teenagers then. They had spent hours at Ruffle's grave, holding hands as Arun rested his head on Maya's shoulder, remembering his pet. They had never imagined life without each other.

She closes the almirah.

'See what I mean?' the voice speaks again. Maya listens to it with a blank look in her eyes. 'But you have grown weak over time. Let me take you to another memory. You were a lot stronger then.'

Maya sits on the bed. The room slowly begins to dissolve into a vacuum of nothingness until a smoky cloud appears before her. It becomes darker and darker and takes the shape of a dining table. One by one, chairs start to appear around it. A window forms behind the table letting the bright, lively light in. She finds herself in her dining hall – just outside her room. It is early morning and the dining table is soaked in the golden light of the rising sun.

'Maya, please have your breakfast,' her mom reminds her for the nth time. Breathing, eating and sleeping are mechanical processes for her now. She is in a perpetual state of agony. It is as if someone is ripping her heart out and shredding it to pieces, repeating the process over and over again. Hell.

She gobbles down her meal when her mom comes and sits beside her.

'Why don't you go out with your friends today?' She pats Maya's head affectionately.

Maya shakes her head.

Her mother gets up and hugs her. 'Beta, you must be strong. Arun would have never liked you to be like this.'

As unexpected as it is, Maya lets out a little laugh. Then her eyes well up. 'You think you understand what Arun would have wanted? You think you understand how I feel?' She goes on, 'No! You understand nothing!' She is yelling now. 'You have no idea what it feels like to have lost the one you love so much. But I do. And I understand why some people want to end their lives. It is because they are drowning in constant, never-ending misery. As if an insect is eating you from the inside and making you hollow, your heart constantly throbbing and fluttering in that void. And you believe that nothing in this world can ever improve your state. You desperately want to end this; you desperately want to get out of it. And the only thing that can end this endless state of pain and worthlessness is death; you come to believe that you can end what you are feeling only if you end your life. And so you kill yourself.'

Maya's mother feels a big lump in her throat. She has to protect her daughter. She has to save her. She can't leave her alone for a single minute now. She is worried sick.

Maya notices the dread in her mother's eyes. She lets out a little laugh and says, 'But don't worry, Mom. I am not going to kill myself. I will never do that. Arun may be dead for the whole world but he will always be alive in my world. No one can snatch away the memories of the time I have spent with him. I will live, for he lives inside me.'

The room dissolves into the same nothingness again as the walls and the furniture disappear one by one. The almirah appears and then the walls of her room with the pictures, the study table with the lamp on it. The space turns into her bedroom. It is night again. The bright morning light is gone. Just the light from the night lamp is illuminating the room.

'You have fought this before,' the voice says, 'and you can do it again.'

7

Sasha

Another night with another stranger

Is Sasha a sadist? A nymphomaniac? A BDSM addict? Is she mentally unstable? Mad? Well, she can count back from hundred to one in less than two minutes, what does that say about her?

It is another usual evening. The smoky bar's dimly lit interiors with colourful neon lights make her believe she is in another world, less ugly and disturbing than the real one. She is sitting at the bar counter. A few drinks down, waiting for an easy prey. Does she want to smack and fuck someone tonight? Maybe not. Maybe she just wants to talk . Harmless, hurtless flirting. Just some teasing. She does not really have to find someone. She knows someone will find her. The low neckline giving a full view of her cleavage, the backless top and short skirt will make sure of that. She is picky about the looks. Why waste time on someone who does not match up to her own looks? She has already ignored four men who made a pass at her. All of them were younger than her – no older than twenty-seven or so. Why did younger men approach her so easily? What was it about older women that made them so cocky? 'She missed her chance.' 'A desperate, horny woman, craving for my sexy, rock-hard cock.' 'How can she resist the sexy muscular body I have built in the gym?' 'She must have an impotent husband to dress like a slut and sit here at a bar waiting for men to fuck her.' Is this what they are thinking?

A man with an athletic build, wearing a tight, thin white shirt sits down next to her and smiles. She smiles back.

'Care for a drink?' he offers.

'Why would I say no?' she says flatly.

The guy orders two drinks.

As the drinks are served, Sasha turns to him and says, 'I am not going to ask your name, and neither am I going to tell you mine.'

'I don't mind that, actually. I just wanted to talk to someone today. And it's always better to talk to strangers. Generally they don't judge you the way people who know you do.'

Sasha takes a longer look at the guy now. He has dark brown eyes and unusually long eyelashes, wearing thin-rimmed round glasses. He is hot, attractive, but not in a raw, purely physical way. He has an appealing softness to him, an underlying sophistication that forces you to be polite to him.

'I wanted to talk to a stranger, that's why I came alone. What about you? Why are you alone?' he asks her.

'I wanted to fuck somebody, that's why I am alone,' she says, straight into his eyes.

'Straightforward and raw. There are not many people like you.'

'You are mistaken, sweetheart, the world is full of people like me. Fewer women, maybe. But men, almost all.' Sasha smiles.

'Almost, but not all.' He was making it so obvious that he was the exception. Crazy little rat.

'Married or single?' Sasha asks.

'Married. You?'

'Does it matter? Does it matter to you?' she replies.

'It does, actually. If you are married, you would be more mature. Seen more of life. I would have more to learn from you.'

How old is he? Five? Why such flattery? Does he think all this boring talk is going to pull her into bed with him?

'Tell me something, why do people marry? I mean . . . isn't it more fun to remain single?'

If Sasha had been as young as him, she would have given some dreamy answer like 'people marry to spend their life with a companion who is their strength, support and reason to live. They marry to fill their life with love.' But life has taught her otherwise. 'Men and women marry for different reasons, I think,' she says after a long silence as bright lights and music pulsate in the background.

'That's a thought. Why do you think women get married?' the guy asks.

Sasha takes a moment to evaluate the man. He is a fine male specimen. Good muscular frame and wearing an attire to intentionally accentuate it.

'Women are complex beings. Each one would give you a different answer for this,' she says

'And what would your answer be?'

'You are suffering from an unhappy marriage,' Sasha states.

'Isn't everyone suffering from that?' he retorts.

'Cut this shit. Tell me, why do men get married?'

'That's a tough one. But I think most men won't get married if they had access to regular sex otherwise.'

Now he is talking. All his 'civilized sophistication' melts away with one plain comment.

'And what about you? Did you also marry for sex?'

'No, actually. In my case, I think it's the other way around. And I am not saying all women are like that, but I think my wife married me for my money and my status. And because . . . she thought . . . she keeps saying that . . . I am too hot . . . sexy . . .' he stammers.

'Wait a minute, you mean to say you feel used for your wealth and sex appeal?'

He nods lightly, avoiding eye contact.

'Then tell me something,' Sasha says as she puts her hand on his chest, lightly caressing it. The top three buttons of his shirt are open. 'If you don't want women to look at you as a sex object, why are you wearing the kind of clothes you are wearing? This semi-transparent, tight shirt that brings attention to your nipples?' she says as she undoes the fourth button. 'Such tight pants that show off your muscular thighs? This properly man-scaped chest hair that runs down to a maintained happy trail?' she says as she runs her hand down to his belly. 'Why are you doing all this? You want girls to find you sexy and that is your aim in life. The irony of the whole thing is that you don't look at women as anything but sex objects and there is nothing else you want to do with them; that is why you have turned yourself into a sex object. You lie that you don't like it but actually it is the sole purpose of your existence – to be a sex object so you can fulfil your needs.'

The guy is stunned. Speechless.

'I can deal with dirty men. I can deal with perverts and corrupt men. But I never waste my time on stupid, hypocritical men.'

The man looks at her in shock. Bright lights and music still on in the background.

'Now, if you will excuse me, I need to find someone to have sex with tonight.' With that, she leaves.

8

Maya

She drags herself on

Happiness is momentary but sadness lasts forever. The effect of something that has made you happy never lasts as long as that of something that made you sad, something that has wrecked your heart and killed a part of you. So much has changed since Arun's death, and yet, so little. Still the sun rises every morning and throws the same shadows and the same rectangular patch of golden light on the floor in my room that moves towards the door and then vanishes. Staring at it I remind myself that everything in this world has a definite life. Things come and go and none of us can hold on to anything forever. Staring at that patch of light, I convince myself that I must live on. But somehow my thoughts violently turn back to Arun. He was the most important part of my life. And when something becomes that big in your life, it changes your whole world. And now my life is just a set of rotting ruins of that world. In the past one year I have experienced a lot. A heartache so strong that it made me run out of breath. I have experienced fame. I have experienced what some might call success. But most of those things were temporary. They floated away as quickly as they came, taking away the contentment they had brought along. Only the grief and a throbbing hollowness remained.

I am repeating my year at college. I had missed enough classes to hold me back a year. Now I attend college every day, without fail. I don't know what I am gaining from it. I just sit there like a log, at times struggling to focus, trying to understand what the teacher is saying. Even if there are any thoughts running in my mind, I am unaware of them. Or I don't remember them as soon as they end in my mind. I have come to understand that I am not sad, but I am just not happy – a state that I don't think I will ever get out of.

I pull out my mobile phone and look at the time. Ten minutes for the class to start. I gather my stuff that is scattered all around me – my charcoal pencils, my pencil pouch and my sketchbook – and put everything in my bag.

'A beauty for the beauty, a rose for the rose.' I look up and see a boy towering above me. He is holding a red rose in his hand which seems to have been plucked from the campus garden.

'Excuse me?'

'This rose, which is pale and dim compared to your beauty . . . it's for you, for this is the only object that I could find to compliment your divine beauty.'

Why does this boy talk so funny? I don't really know what to say. I sit there, silent. He puts the rose next to my feet and keeps looking at me. He is waiting for my response, waiting for the one specific kind of response that he wants from me. But I don't give him any. Because I don't really feel anything.

'For what it's worth, this one flower has cost me a thousand bucks. I plucked it from this garden. Please accept this as a small token of my love for you, my lady.' He bows.

After another few seconds of awkward silence, he holds my hand and shakes it, 'The world has named me Garun.'

His action is strange. Any other girl, any of my friends would have been amused. But somehow it does not have any effect on me. There is nothing in this world that can shock me any more. He keeps looking into my eyes and then says, 'If I have offended you by touching your hand, let me atone for my sin by kissing it.' He plants a light kiss on the back of my hand and then lets it go.

After a few more awkward moments, I say, 'Are you done?'

'Yes, my lady.' He bows again.

I get up and leave. I do not touch the flower.

When I reach my seat in the classroom, the one where I sit every day like a corpse, I see the same flower on the table. I pick it up and twirl it in my hand. It's red with a hint of pink around the edges of its petals. It's from the bush in the college garden that says '*Fine on plucking flowers: Rs 1000.*' As I look at the rose blankly, I remember the boy's face. I remember his naughty boyish charm.

9

Garun

How will he ever make her fall in love?

I made my first move today. This bitch is gonna be tougher than I thought. She did not respond the way I expected her to. For a moment I suspected she was not into guys at all, maybe she was a lesbian. But then I remembered she had a boyfriend and used to suck his dick. This is gonna take more patience that I thought. But the good thing is that people are already talking about me and her. Some are saying that I had a bet with my friends that I will fuck her. People are dumbasses. What do they think it is, 1920? Even Tarush was asking me about it. He said he knew I wanted to have sex with her, brag about it and then dump her. It makes me want to laugh. All the people around me are so mediocre.

They can never think big. They have no idea what my plan is and they will never be able to guess with their puny, limited minds. I am the best writer this country has ever seen and soon I'll be so famous that the whole world will be licking my feet. I just need to make this whore, Maya, fall for me. Make her feel for me. Love me. Love me so much that I become a part of her life, and then her sole existence.

10

Sasha

The dream life!

What happened to her was a very common tale, but what it made of her was something quite unusual.

Her husband is back from a two-week trip from Europe. He had gone to sign a multi-million-dollar deal with a top-notch car manufacturing company. He had succeeded. What is the total worth of the empire he has created? The figure of $64,500 billion is so mind-boggling that most won't even know how to write it down or how many zeros it has.

His equation with his wife is one you will find in many an Indian home – the husband earns the bread and the social status and demands to be served by his wife. Today he is back after a long, successful business trip and he wants his wife to serve him better than ever. With this new deal, Sasha can buy a necklace with the biggest diamonds she can imagine. Isn't this every woman's dream come true – gold and jewels, big bungalows, luxury cars, clothes so expensive that a small family can run their household for a whole year for the amount?

He is the provider, he is the king and so he stands in front of Sasha like one, almost ordering her to serve him. She knows well what to do. She starts unbuttoning his shirt, starting from the top. Slipping the shirt off his shoulders, she unbuckles his black leather belt, unbuttons his trousers, unzips them and drops them on the floor. His boxers are still on but his hard-on is well visible. She pulls his boxers down. Now it is her turn to undress herself and she can do it any way she likes. Her husband is not particular about the order in which she undresses. He does not care as long as she is naked by the end of it. Sasha sees her husband erect before her, tight and stiff, like a wrestler waiting for the whistle to start the rumble. She puts her hands on his shoulders and runs them down his chest, his belly, to his waist and his thighs. She knows how to keep her touch gentle and sensuous. Her husband is at the peak of excitement now. He holds Sasha by the shoulders and pulls her up. A silent moment and a deep gaze into each other's eyes. No words but a lot said in a matter of seconds. He cups her breasts and rubs his knee against her thigh. He hugs her, rather squeezes her tight. Sasha hugs him back, resting her chin on his shoulder. He starts thrusting his pelvis against her and that is when she notices the mark on his back – a hickie, a love bite. He had been with another, he had fucked another woman, again, during his trip. But this does not upset her; she does not feel betrayed the way she had when she discovered that the man she had married was not really a 'one-woman man'.

Their marriage was eight months old when it had happened. Their daughter was a six-month-old fetus in her uterus. She was furious, she wanted a divorce. His argument was that he had to go away for long business trips she couldn't accompany him on due to her pregnancy. But he had physical needs that had to be fulfilled. Her parents were upset to hear about it but convinced her to stay. 'He has gone astray, you are his wife, you have to teach him the right way,' they had told her, as if it was the 1950s. But things didn't change. Instead of teaching her husband, she learned that this was how things rolled for the rich and the famous.

Her husband is inside her now. She stares at the love mark on his back for a while and then lifts her head. She kisses his shoulder and starts sucking on it. She wants to leave a mark darker than the one on his back.

After the long, passionate sex, they are both on the bed. Her husband falls into a deep sleep within minutes but she stays awake, lying on her back, staring at the ceiling. She is silent on the outside but raging mad inside. She wants to hit her husband. She wants to make him fall to his knees and beg for mercy. But she can't do any of that. He is the reason for her existence after all – he is the one because of whom she has the status and the respect she enjoys socially. Without him she is nothing. But she has to let her fury out. She has to find another man. She has to thrash one, whip one and kick one in the balls.

What happened to her was a very common tale, but what that made of her was something quite unusual.

11

Garun

The pickup artist

I go to the gym only in the evenings for a reason. I pump up my body so that I look sexy when I go to the club. Today was chest and biceps day and my muscles are hard as rock. And if I have learned anything over the years, it is that chicks love the feel of hard muscle. It's eight o'clock – the perfect time to hit the disc and pick up a girl.

I push the door open and the big bouncer nods and lets me in. He knows I am a regular. They change the colour of the lighting for this place every week. Today they have blue and red lights flashing alternately giving the whole place an out of the world kind of feel.

I go directly to the loo to check myself out in the mirror. My hair looks perfect. Stubble just as it should be – the three-day look suits my face best. Shoulders, chest and biceps solid and pumped. Shirt tucked in perfectly to hint at my six-pack. I open the top four buttons of my shirt and give myself a wink in the mirror. I look like a total killer today. Girls are gonna freak out and run after me the moment they see me. I step out of the loo and a group of three girls pass me by. One of them is wearing a black dress and looks upset. 'This neckline is just not working for me. It's just too high.' She is pouting in disappointment. 'It does not even touch my cleavage. I *need* to be noticed. It *needs* to show how round, firm and smooth I am. This dress is terrible! It does nothing to accentuate my figure. God! My whole *evening* is ruined!' She is on the verge of tears.

We have just the right crowd today. I love girls in this vulnerable state. They would do anything to attract you. You can make them do anything you want.

I move to the counter and place my order. The mug of frothy beer placed on the counter for me makes my mouth water. I take a swig and the cold, refreshing beer runs down my throat, giving me divine pleasure, refreshing my senses. I close my eyes for a moment to hold the feeling.

'One beer, please.' I hear a girl's voice as I open my eyes and turn to look at her. It's the same girl I saw going into the loo earlier. She has changed her clothes. She is now dressed in some kind of printed chiffon, and it is a lot shorter, revealing more than her cleavage. I need some action tonight. My hunter needs to do some hunting. This chick is hot. I must give it a try. Let's see what she is looking for.

I smile at her and nod. She smiles and turns back to her drink. Good! She is interested. I know her kind. Fifteen minutes and she will be ready to go with me where I want to take her.

'You look beautiful,' I say.

She rolls her eyes with a hint of embarrassment. She is new, fresh to this whole business. 'Tell me something I don't know,' she says, trying to tease me with eyes heavily laden with eye shadow, mascara and eyeliner, making her look like she is meant for only one purpose – to be fucked and thrown away.

'What I meant was, you look hot, *sexy*.'

She smiles and extends her hand for a handshake. 'Ankita.'

'Vishal.' I always take care never to tell my real name. You never know what kind of a bitch she may turn out to be.

'How's your evening been so far?' I try to initiate conversation.

'Pretty lousy.' She makes a face as she stirs her beer with her index finger, making sure we have eye contact as she licks it like a porn actor.

I smile to make her comfortable. I look around and see her two friends sitting with two other guys in two different corners of the hall, throwing their heads back and laughing like sluts.

'Alone or with friends?' I ask.

'Alone,' she lies.

'Great! It's so much better to be alone, on your own.'

'I *know*!' she says, her eyes popping out, almost spurting out the beer she has just sipped. 'And if you were to spend time with your friends, you might as well just call them over and stay at home, no? God! That is such a loser thing to do.'

'I know.' I laugh and I raise my hand for a high five.

'Do you like this place? It's not really my favourite,' I say.

'I don't mind it.' She takes another swig of her drink.

'There is another place close by. Must have heard about Cleavages, sorry, I mean Claridges,' I say.

She bursts out laughing, and puts her hand on her mouth in the most pretentiously delicate way. Her nails are long and French manicured. She is wearing a ring in her little finger from which a thin gold chain hangs loosely. I can't make out more details in the dim light.

I shift in my chair, pretend to be embarrassed and give an awkward smile.

'It's okay, really. So you were saying, Hotel Cleavages.'

'Hotel Claridges . . . has a really great bar. If you like, we can go there. It's a thousand times better than this place.

'Sure! Why not.' She laughs. Not sure if it's her drink hitting her or my slip of the tongue.

I am set. This girl is gonna be my bitch tonight. This slut was easier than I thought. I run a quick mental calculation of the money I have in my wallet. I think I have some 20k for the night. It's a good figure for tonight but that's all I have left for the month. After this if I want another bitch to suck my horn, I will need more money. I need to find a way to make good money soon or it will be tough to have a good life.

'Shall we go?' I offer her my hand.

'Thank you.' She smiles, taking my hand, probably imagining herself to be some kind of stupid princess from those lame-ass romcoms. I put my arm around her exposed shoulder and caress it. 'It's a little cold outside,' I say.

'Is okay, I have you to keep me warm,' she says as she flashes another smile at me.

~

Garun turns the key to his prized apartment. As soon as he pushes the door open, he hears a loud, annoying flutter of wings inside. He quickly scans the hall with hawk-like eyes. He must have left the bathroom window open when he left in the morning. A pigeon has entered his apartment. It is not the first time this has happened. He can't let this ugly bird stay inside. It will create the greatest mess. According to him, these creatures have no right to live on the face of this earth. They are one of the many useless creatures who breathe and move on this planet and should have gone extinct before humans evolved and took over the world. Maybe some day some wise scientists will devise a way to wipe out the existence of all such animals. As much as he hates a dumb bird being trapped in his house, he enjoys what he does to them. Just the thought of that brings an evil smile on Garun's face. He looks at the pigeon flying around in circles, panicking at the intrusion of a two-legged monster in the space where it had not been disturbed all day. After a few minutes the pigeon finally settles on the open bedroom door and poops. This only infuriates Garun. This means that the bird will suffer a crueller death than Garun had planned for it just a few moments ago. Wide-eyed, the pigeon looks around with swift jerks of the neck. Garun moves to the switchboard with the cautious steps of a cat and switches off the light.

The pigeon is clutched tight in his hand when Garun goes and switches on the lights in the kitchen. He takes a nylon thread and winds it around the bird, binding its wings to kill any kind of movement. He places it on its back on the kitchen counter. He grabs a pair of heavy, sharp tailor's scissors and runs it a few times up in the air above the bird as it looks back at him in horror, struggling in its futile attempt to break free.

Garun looks at the bird and smiles. He is getting a high from the mere thought of what he is going to do to it.

'Don't worry, kid, your misery won't last long. You will be dead in less than fifteen minutes from now.' He looks at the wall clock and then back at the bird with the smile still fixed on his face.

He holds its leg with one hand and first clips the claws. This action is more or less painless for the bird but when he chops off its toes, one by one, the bird cries out as blood flows from what is left of its feet – which now look like dried twigs of a bush. The room echoes with the crazy shrieks of the bird.

'Bad, ill-mannered bird you are!' he says to the pigeon. 'Such a terrible, ugly noise you are making. Wait, let me put on some music.'

He wipes his bloody hands with a kitchen towel, connects his phone to his Bluetooth speakers and plays a song. The sound of crashing guitars and loud drums drown out the helpless cries of the bird. He settles down by the table again. 'Yes, much better,' he says as if the bird could understand him.

He holds the pigeon's body down with one hand and smiles at it viciously. What he is about to do now is the part he enjoys the most. He grabs the leg of the bird with the other hand, tightens his grip and pulls the leg out with one swift jerk. He watches with great pleasure as a tiny red fountain springs up and fills the empty socket. Within seconds, the other leg of the pigeon is gone too. With the deafening music playing, he only sees the pigeon jerking its neck frantically. Its shrieks only seem to be a part of the orchestra of the song. Garun picks up the bird again, unwinds the nylon thread and plucks out its wing feathers one by one. After this tedious task it is time for the final act. He lòoks at the wall clock again. This whole process has taken exactly twelve minutes.

'I told you,' he says looking down at the bird, 'it would take less than fifteen minutes. I am not as cruel as you think.'

He holds the head of the pigeon in his hand and gripping it tight, gives it a 360-degree twist. And then he keeps twisting the head round and round, long after the bird is dead. Long after the spinal cord has snapped, the body lifeless, with no signals or electrical impulses running through it.

He wipes the table clean with a spotless white cotton cloth. Putting the pieces of the dead bird into a plastic bag, he disposes it of into the dustbin. After washing the blood off his hands, he goes into his room. The room looks as if it has been transported right from his old, tiny two-bedroom apartment. All the posters – *Dexter*, *Game of Thrones*, *The Walking Dead* – are almost in the same positions as they were in his former, smaller room. He lives on these shows. There is just one addition in the room – a spider in a glass case. Garun has a thing for insects. He finds their discipline and organization admirable – from ants to bees, on land or in air. He finds there is no laziness in them. If ever questioned or asked to explain, he would say, 'They are always active and smart. Try observing an ant sometime, how it tirelessly carries its food. How it does not even wait for its host to die before scraping out tiny chunks of meat. Ever seen ants consume a lizard? So efficient, so quick.' Spiders, however, are his favourite. How very patiently they weave a flawless web – the best trap one can ever devise – visible and invisible in its own way. How they wait for their prey so patiently. They know that sooner or later the prey will walk into the trap due to its own stupidity. Humans have a lot to learn from this insect, he feels.

He looks at his pet inside the glass case and taps lightly. The spider moves. Garun smiles. 'The little beast is hungry,' he says. He opens the big jar of flies placed next to the spider case and puts two flies in for the spider, quickly closing the lid back so that the flies can't escape. He peeps into the spider case again as the flies buzz around bumping against the glass. 'Enjoy, my little friend,' he says and continues to peer into the glass case.

12

Maya

A thousand questions

What is life? What is its meaning? What does not have a purpose can never exist. What is our purpose? How significant are we? What should matter to us? Nothing is important or of any significance. But at the same time everything is. We ourselves and the people around us are so small, so insignificant that in the wide cosmos we don't matter at all. But another truth is that we and all the people around us make all the difference for us. Are we, humans, capable of accepting and living by the truths of existentialism? Arun was just another human being like a billion others. Does the absence of one human being make any difference to the world? My friends, the people who know me, say that I have changed completely after Arun passed away. That I am not the same person any more. Is it so? Does the old Maya still exist? Or is she dead? Did she die along with Arun, the day he drew his last breath? And if Maya is dead, does this mean she has transcended to the same world to which Arun had gone? Does this mean now she can meet him again? The mere thought is comforting beyond belief.

13

Garun

Like a moth to a flame

The ball flies towards me and I kick it, sending it towards the goal. Another guy from my team takes over. It's enough football practice for today. I am drenched in sweat. I pull off my shirt and wipe myself. From the corner of my eye I see Maya sitting at the edge of the field – her usual spot. I have been following her like a shadow. I know her exact routine. What time she comes to college, what time she leaves, where she sits to have her food, where she sits and sketches during the free slots in the timetable. Right now she should have been checking me out and admiring my smouldering hot body but instead she is busy putting some ugly black pencil marks in her sketchbook. I have to make her notice how well cut I am. I need to tempt her physical desires. Every human craves to touch and feel another body and especially when the body is as hot as mine. Bare-chested, with my football jersey clutched in my hand, I walk up to her.

'Hi.'

She looks up briefly and drops her gaze back to her sketchbook. She continues sketching and only gives a quick nod to acknowledge my presence. I did catch a glimpse of discomfort when she looked at me and quickly put my shirt on. God help me! She is one of those behenji types. I need to switch to Plan B. I kneel down in front of her.

'I . . . don't know how to start,' I stammer.

She just sits there silently as if I don't even exist.

'I . . . really wanted to apologize for my behaviour the other day.'

Silence

'I should not have behaved the way I did and I am really, really sorry for that.'

'It's okay,' comes her flat, emotionless reply.

'Thank you. But in my defence, I acted that way because you are really, really beautiful. And I firmly believe that any potent man would be blown away by your beauty. Cannot take his eyes off you without killing his desire to get close to you.'

She looks up, puts her pencil on her sketchbook and says, 'What is all this about?' She is irritated.

'It's all about you and the importance of your smile. I want you to smile.'

She shoots me a hard stare and then goes back to sketching.

I peep into her sketchbook. I see some ugly scribbles.

'Your art resembles Candela Blanca Cuervo.'

The mere mention of Candela makes her pencil halt. This is it! I have caught her pulse now. Good I did some homework about this trashy charcoal artist that the whole world worships.

'Yeah, I mean just look how you round off each of your strokes. That is so definitely Candela Blanca Cuervo.'

For the first time, a trace of a smile appears on her face and then it vanishes again.

'Cut the chase and tell me what you want. Generally your kind talk to girls only because they have some crazy bets with their friends and stuff.'

'Not in my case, my lady. And my desire is very plain and simple – I only want to be friends with you.'

'Why?' she fires back.

It's working. She is talking. 'I have been observing you for a while, Maya. And I don't like to see you so sad all the time–'

'I am not sad, I am just not happy.'

'Yes, you are sad.'

'No, I am not.'

'Okay, fine. Then tell me why you are not happy. What is wrong?'

'I am sorry but I don't discuss my life with strangers.'

'Okay, fine, then let's not be strangers. And since I know pretty well that you won't tell me anything about yourself or ask me any questions, I take on the responsibility to alter my status from "a stranger" to "someone known". As I mentioned earlier, my name is Garun. I live in Gurugram, did my schooling from Ting Tong International School. Have one sole aim in life and that is to become the biggest living author in the world. So far I have only been focused on my studies, never been in a relationship, no girlfriend whatsoever, but now that I am in this good college and my future seems to be a little secure, I am open to the idea. They say that journeys end when lovers meet. I want to see how it feels when a journey ends. I was a very studious kid in school. Did no wrong. I think I am destined to have one partner for life. When I have a girlfriend, I want her to be with me for life. I want to grow old with her and spend the rest of my life with her.'

'You want to be a writer?' she asks.

'Yes ma'am, I do.' I nod like a cowboy from one of those old Westerns.

'You know I have written a novel?' She has a strange way of talking. She does not look at me as she talks.

'Yes, I do.' I smile. 'And I loved it. I've never read such an honest account of feelings before.'

'So that means that you practically know almost everything about me.'

'Well, if what you have written in the book is your own life, then, yes, but . . . that book is fiction, no?' I enquire.

'All fiction is sucked out of reality. No such thing as pure fiction exists in this world.'

She has started talking. This is good.

'So you have read my book and you know what happened to me and yet you want me to be happy?'

I look her in the eyes intensely. 'Maya, whatever happened was not your fault. I know it's unfair on my part to comment on any of this because I cannot feel what you have felt and are going through, but what I know is that every wound heals with time. It may leave some scars but the pain eventually goes away.'

She is looking back at me. She is listening.

'Maya, you are a very nice person. You are as beautiful from the inside as you are on the outside. And people like you deserve to be happy. I will make sure you are as happy and cheerful as you said you used to be in your book.'

14

Maya

Crash! Boom! Bang!

My whole body is still trembling from the shock of what just happened. I am sitting in the living room with my hands clasped tight on my lap. When I rang the doorbell and Mom opened the door, she was so alarmed at my state that she almost screamed. My hair was all messed up. My face had scratches and patches of dried blood. Bruises and stains of dirt and grease. She put her arm around my shoulder and brought me in and made me sit on the sofa. Then she rushed to the kitchen to get me a glass of water. She sat down next to me and gently asked me what had happened.

I broke down in a fit of sobs. 'I met with an accident.' I shut my eyes tight but they could not contain the tears. 'I met with an accident,' I repeated and cried.

~

Mom has been extremely worried about me ever since my return from the hospital. She has been trying her best to cheer me up. She has been cooking my favourite dishes, getting me small gifts from every trip to the market. She has seen all her efforts fail but she refuses to give up. This morning she asked if I wanted to go out for a drive. I did not really but refusing would have got her upset and given her incentive to come up with another bad idea to make me feel better. I took the keys.

I drove around aimlessly for a while, not caring where I was going, just taking one turn after another, passing one vehicle after another. As if I was on autopilot. It was only after some time that I realized what was happening. I was going round and round, on the route which Arun used to take me for a drive on every evening. And then all those evenings spent with him flashed in front of my eyes. The spot where I would always beg for an ice cream but he would let me have it only on Saturdays, the street vendor who prepared the best noodle-burger, everything was right there. I could not take it any more. I wanted to bring my car to a screeching halt and cry. But I held strong. When a tear escaped one eye I wiped it off with the back of my hand. I kept driving. Then I had a strange feeling that someone was sitting in the back seat, looking at me. I turned around and could not believe my eyes. It was Arun smiling lovingly at me. I blinked, he was still there. I blinked again and he was gone. I blinked once more and he was there again. Suddenly I heard a loud horn honking. The sound was rushing towards me. I turned to find a car speeding towards me. I was in the wrong lane. I turned the wheel with a quick hand. The honking continued as the car rushed past me. I sighed in relief and then remembered what I had just seen. I turned back again but there was no one there. I turned my gaze to the road again. I wanted to go home. I was dizzy. My throat was suddenly bone dry. Just then everything in front of me became cloudy. I blinked and squinted. My vision was sharp again but after a while the road in front of me split into four. It was a strange feeling. Was I in a new place? I could not figure out. I drove on as the four roads merged into one and after a few seconds split again. And then I felt a massive jerk. Everything around me started to melt like wax and I noticed the tree into which my car had crashed. I was safe but the windscreen had shattered, its pieces rained all over me. Scratches on my knuckles. Scratches on my forehead. Some scratches on my ears.

My mother is sitting next to me, hugging and rocking me like I am a baby. She whispers lightly, 'Thank God you are safe,' and kisses me on my head. This is all she says but I know there's a lot more going on in her mind. She is blaming herself for sending me out for a drive. She is blaming herself for putting my life in danger and almost losing me. She has certainly decided she'll never let me drive again.

15

Garun

Fishing a story

It's working. She finally opened her trap today. I could almost see her spreading her legs with her two lips in the middle craving my meat as she talked, imagining herself to be the biggest intellectual on earth. God! She is so lame. 'All fiction is sucked from reality' my ass! I don't know which sorry book she read that quote from and 'chepoed' on me today. The only thing she is actually capable of sucking is my dick.

Anyway, my plan is working now. I have got her hooked on to me. All fiction is sucked from reality she says, is it? Well, I am gonna suck out a story from her. I am gonna take over her life, give it the most amazing twists and turns and write a 'true story' about it. That is what people love to read – stories about helpless, grief-stricken girls who should have been dead long ago, if you ask me. Everyone loves a sob story. I am gonna suck one out of this whore and throw it in front of the world. Oh God! This is so exciting. I can't wait for things to get rolling now. But the only problem is that I can't get her in my bed so soon. I need to wait. Make other arrangements. My bank account has run dry, I've exhausted the money I got from my books. I need to find a way to make more soon.

16

Maya

The mystical reunion

I wander in the desert of my loneliness where the faint shadow of your voice follows me, always. I thought you had left me forever, Arun. I thought I would never see you again but I know you were with me that day in the car. My eyes couldn't have lied to me. And I know your voice is following me. It is your voice I have been hearing. At times I can almost feel you sitting next to me. I knew you would never leave me alone. I knew if I couldn't leave this world and join you, you would come back for me. I stand in front of the mirror. I was never a pretty kid. I had a fat and ugly nose. I still do. Kids used to call me the Wicked Witch of the East. We were in fourth standard then. One of my classmates made a little postcard with an ugly face of a witch on it. Nose as big as her face. Teeth, crooked. I saw it but pretended to have missed it and slipped it down on the floor. I wanted to behave as if nothing had happened but after a few seconds I started crying. You noticed that, Arun. You quickly made a little drawing – a smiling girl with two pretty little ponytails, an arrow pointing to her with the words 'my little princess, Princess Maya' – and placed it on my desk. It made me smile. Then you made another drawing, one of Medusa, with snakes for hair, spreading in all directions and labelled it 'Sunaina' – the girl who had put the drawing on my desk before. You asked me to pass you that ugly little postcard and you had ripped it to shreds. You were the only one who saw me as beautiful. You gave me the confidence to face the world. Thoughts of you, Arun, of the times I spent with you during my childhood make me smile.

I am smiling into the mirror. Slowly, my face begins to wobble. The mirror begins to ripple like water does when a stone is dropped into it, first slowly and then rapidly, till the ripples suddenly vanish. I don't realize when it starts but my nose begins to grow. It keeps expanding like a balloon, till it covers my whole face. I look monstrously, hideously ugly. I cannot bear to see it. I shut my eyes tight.

'No!' I scream and turn away.

I am frozen for a while and then slowly turn towards

the mirror again. I keep staring. I have lost my thoughts, all of them. Suddenly I am no one, I have no character, no personality. Then I notice smoke appearing in front of me. It changes from black to grey to blue to green to orange to red to yellow to blue. It keeps growing and expanding, gaining volume. All my thoughts and memories are there in that haze, in that cloud that has formed. That cloud is everything I know, it is everything I am. It is all of my being, that cloud is me. All my thoughts and memories, moving in the haze, have jumbled into a huge ball, a cloud with the hazy, moving images of all the memories in it. The cloud slowly starts to turn into golden text floating in the air. Then the words merge together into a solid shining metal ball. It floats out of the mirror, steadily moving towards me. It comes to a halt right in front of my face. I can see my distorted reflection on its golden surface as if I am looking through a fish-eye lens. It stays there for a while and then moves again. It gently eases into my forehead. The ball is inside my head now, in place of my brain, but I can still see it. My head feels heavy. Very heavy. So heavy that I have to support it with my hand to keep my neck from snapping. Pain shoots through my body. Sharp, unbearable, excruciating. The headache is piercing. I shut my eyes tight. I must not scream again. I bite my lower lip hard. I don't want to cut myself, I don't want to bleed. I don't want to have a visible wound that would arouse suspicion. But the pain is too much. And then, in less than a fraction of a second, it is gone. My head feels normal, light again. I feel normal. But the room still feels strange. Something is different. It takes me a while to figure it out. There is a fragrance in the room which was not there a few seconds ago. I know this fragrance. It is the perfume Arun used to wear. I look around wildly. Is he here? Is he with me in this room?

'Arun would have never wanted you to be this way. This sad, this disturbed. You know that well. Why can't you just do this for him?' It's that voice again. I look at my pillow. It is back – that line, that strand of hair on my white pillow, vibrating and moving, talking to me again. 'You know this. I brought it back to you in that memory I showed you. Why do you not follow it?'

I am dumbstruck.

'Would you do it if he came back? Would you keep your promise then?'

I nod. My mouth twitches and my eyes well up. 'Yes,' I say, shutting my eyes tight. 'Yes,' as tears stream down my face, my neck. 'Yes.' I collapse on the floor, breaking into a fit of sobs. It is the only sound in the room. Bent over with my forehead on the floor, I can see the pools of my tears growing bigger. Then suddenly I hear it.

'Hello Maya.'

My sobs come to an abrupt stop. The voice makes me forget everything that's happened even a second ago. My wet eyes are wide open. Arun.

I look up. It is him. He is standing in front of the closed door of my room. He is here. *He is real.*

17

Sasha

Grabbing (life) by the balls 1

The man is much younger than her, strong and muscular. One of those fit all-rounders whom everyone admires in office. She had found him delicious when she first saw him, all suited-booted in crisp formals. They got talking over a drink where he could not stop boasting about his achievements – all the countries he had already visited at such a young age, his impressive bank balance and how he was so good in bed that every woman wanted to sleep with him more than once. He was a free spirit, he said, he grabbed life by the balls and lived it to the fullest. He said his life changed after watching that Bollywood movie shot in Spain, in which three friends realize the value of life during their trip.

After having dragged the overly excited man by his thin necktie to the hotel room, Sasha had merely begun extracting her pleasure from his body when he started crying out in pain. Although he was gagged to mute any sounds escaping his throat, his horrified eyes were bloodshot and cheeks wet from tears as he lay with his limbs tied to the bed. Just a few kicks to his balls and his dick shrank and went limp as a dead lizard. With eyes popping out like bulbs, he shook his head violently. She could hear the muffled 'nos' and 'stops' over and over again. She was disgusted. This man could not even take the slightest of pain. She wanted to torture him even more. But experience had taught her that it was best to let such men go. God had created them weak, even physically, contrary to their appearance. She had pushed one such man beyond his limit once and it had turned out very messy. Not only did she have blood, piss and shit all over the fine satin sheets, the man had passed out and had to be taken to hospital. That one session had cost her a lot more than she had expected. She had to cover up, pay a lot of people to close the matter. She does not want such a mess again.

She unties the man. He sits up, wiping his tears, too shocked and scared to say anything. Men in their mid-twenties are no more courageous than mice. Sasha walks over to the side table where her expensive crocodile skin bag is kept and pulls out a bundle of notes. She throws it on the man's face, grabs his hair, pulls his head back and hisses, 'Take this, and never show me your face again.'

The man avoids eye contact. He picks up the money and starts dressing himself. His failure to endure the pain, his weakness pisses her even further. She marches to her bag and pulls out a pair of scissors. She grabs his pants and slits them right through the crotch. The man is so shocked that he wants to scream but his vocal chords fail him. He wets his pants.

'Get out!' she yells. 'GET OUT!'

The man gathers all his clothes and runs out of the room, leaving the door open. Sasha storms to the door and shuts it with a loud bang. Her elegant body, as always, is covered only by a thin black chiffon gown. She slumps on the couch by the window and lights her cigar. Her hands shake for a bit. The face of the young man writhing in pain flashes in front of her eyes. His teeth clenching due to the pain, his eyes wide with horror. His eyes. There was innocence in them.

Those eyes have a lot more of this world to see before his outlook changes to one as ugly as her own. Sasha has become a monster, an ugly wreck of a person. And she wants everyone to be like her. She wants to hurt everyone. When she was younger, the same age as the man whose nuts she has just busted, she would never have imagined she'd turn into the person she is now.

Back then, everyone told her she would be famous one day.

'But I don't think I want to be famous,' she had told her friend, Monica.

'Oh come on! Everyone wants to be famous. Don't lie. You are not standing before a panel of judges at a beauty pageant.' The two had been friends since their first day at college. Usually people shed the first set of friends they make upon joining college, but Sasha and Monica were exceptions to that trend. They had hit it off the moment they met, worked as team members in various projects and assignments, and gone through the raging days together.

'I don't think being famous would make me feel special. I don't think it's a feeling as strong as love or hate or loneliness. It doesn't come from within; it is not generated by the heart or mind. Rather, it is something external, something that stems from the minds of others and is thrown at us,' Sasha explained.

'Don't throw all this stupid philosophy at me. I don't know about you but *I* want to be famous, someone the world is crazy about, someone the paparazzi chase all the time!'

'Trust me, Monica, you don't.' Sasha smiled.

'I don't know about myself, but, as for you, I am certain you will be famous one day. I mean . . . have you even seen your work? Your paintings are pure genius.

Even the teachers can't deny that. You always get an A+ on all your submissions. You are going to give tough competition to artists like M.F. Husain and Subodh Gupta. You are going to be famous, you just don't realize what you are capable of. I don't know why you underestimate yourself so much.'

'It's not about underestimating myself, but, anyway, leave it.'

Sitting on that couch, Sasha remembers her college days as a tear rolls down her cheek. Sometimes happy memories stab us more painfully than sad ones. She was in her final year when she had got married. Two months later she had got pregnant. A few months later she had realized that her marriage was not based on love or affection. She has not quit painting. Her art, which was all about fantastic, playful lines and colours right out of wonderland, now only depicts pain, blood, fire and torment, directed at people and the world. The wonderland has turned into a nightmarish hell.

18

Garun

Grabbing (life) by the balls 2

There is a middle-aged woman ahead of us in the corridor, dragging a much younger man by his necktie, teasing him, making sure he has a hard-on by the time they reach their room. The room they step into is right opposite ours. As the odd couple enters the room, I make brief eye contact with the woman. There is an unearthly, devilish glint in her eyes. She looks at me and her lips curl into an evil smile. I shut the door and turn around. The girl that I have picked up at the bar today is hot. She swings her expensive Gucci bag as she walks to the window for a view of the nightscape.

'Nice room you have booked.' She turns around and smiles. She is so drunk she can barely stand straight.

'Anything for someone as special as you.' I move closer to her. 'Would you like to order something to eat?'

'Umm, not really. Are you hungry?' She is trying her best to be all chirpy.

'Not right now. But I guess in some time we will be hungry.' I smile.

'Umm.' She pouts and smiles.

I turn on the TV and surf the channels. There is a special channel called 'Erotic' for the likes of us. It shows me a list of movies on offer. After a quick browse I select the one called *Seduction Hotel*.

'This one looks good,' I call out. She is standing by the window, still peering out.

'Huh, what?' She turns around.

'I found a nice movie on TV.'

'Which one? Which one?' She runs towards me.

'It's called *Seduction Hotel*.' I take her in my arms.

She giggles. 'Sounds like the hotel we are in.' She runs her hand down my jeans and strokes me, just enough to turn my kid into a roaring lion. I like this girl. I throw her on to the bed. She looks up at me with greedy, playful eyes, but doesn't make the first move. I lean in and start kissing her, slowly at first, just to make her comfortable, then I start smooching her hard. I move my hands over her body, feeling her breasts, then slowly making my way down. She starts unbuttoning my shirt. I get up and take it off all the way. I help her slip off her dress, leaving her smooth skin naked. Now she is only wearing a lacy, see-through bra and slutty panties. I run my fingers over her panties and she is already wet. I like that. I bend down and caress her neck while my hands work on her bra. I struggle for a bit when I feel her hands over mine, helping me take it off. This girl is a real score. She is completely naked now, while I am still in my denims. She wildly climbs on top of me. I am almost hard. She bites my lower lip and then my neck. Her nails graze my chest as she moves down to my navel. She unbuttons my jeans, takes them off along with my boxers. I lie there staring at her, half erect. She sucks on my navel while rubbing my dick with her hand, teasing me. She moves down soon, puts my dick in her mouth and sucks it hard, giving me a full erection. I am completely charged up and just want to fuck her. I pull her up by her hair. Grabbing her by the waist I turn her over. I suck her right nipple and massage her pussy with my middle finger. I suck her breast till it feels raw. I move up and push my dick inside her. She moans and it excites me even more. The harder I move, the louder she moans. Her breasts move up and down and I grab and squeeze them hard just as I am about to come.

~

We are done in less than an hour. After that there is nothing really left to do. She is just a perfect, dumb bimbo, completely incapable of maintaining any kind of conversation for over a minute. Her pussy talks a lot better than the pair of lips on her mouth. I want to leave. I don't want to spend the whole night here but she has passed out. Why did the bitch drink so much? Next time I need to keep a tab on the number of drinks we order before I get such sluts to bed. I pull out a cigarette from my bag and light it, take a drag and puff out a circular ring of smoke that slowly rises in front of me. I think about my situation. I am lying naked next to a naked girl with a perfect body on the white sheets on a bed in an expensive hotel. This is the life I have always dreamt of. There is hardly anything I can complain about. My eyes are focused on the ring of smoke, rising, expanding. I blow out another one and watch it follow the one above it. I look at the girl fast asleep with her back towards me. The satin bed sheet is lightly resting on her thighs, leaving her perfect round ass exposed. The line of her backbone, visible, dipping slightly above her hips, curved and arched up to terminate between her shoulder blades. I trace a line on her back with my fingers. She is so fast asleep that she does not even feel my touch. This is what a man lives for. These are the fine pleasures of life, the experiences that we have been sent to earth for. One girl after another, I need someone to fuck. But I am running out of money. I pull out my wallet to check my cash. Shit! I don't even have enough to hire a cab home in the morning. I need to find a way to make quick money. I would do anything for it. Just then I remember something. The face of the woman I saw in the corridor. Her eyes and her evil smile flash once again in front of my eyes. She was with a younger man. They were clearly going to have sex. They seemed to have met a few hours ago. I am sure they had not known each other before. That woman was definitely a crazy sex addict. A married, unhappy, unsatisfied wrench spreading her legs for strangers. She looked rich, someone who had money to throw at anyone to make him sleep with her. Maybe these are the kind of women I need to use. I should give such women some hard sex and earn some money out of it. There must be a lot of women out there who would pay for a well-built, hot boy like me. This is it. This is exactly what I need. These rich bitches, they will pay me as much as I ask for once they taste my cum. I will give them what their faggot, impotent husbands are not giving them – a good, satisfying fuck. All I need is to find a way to reach out to them. And these days reaching out to people is not difficult at all. Once they have a taste of me, they will want me again and again. I need to get a web page up and running to get in touch with such needy whores. Get the right keywords and some search engine optimization. And when it comes to fucking and sex, finding the keywords is never a problem. God, this is brilliant. I love it.

19

Maya

In dreams, on the magic carpet

Last night I stumbled upon a lost memory of you in my mind. Of the golden days when you used to make me sit in front of you and to paint me on your canvas. It would go on for hours. I would not even have a thread covering my body but it never made me uncomfortable. I remember how shy I was when you asked me to undress for you the first time. I didn't understand what you wanted. I doubted you. You said if I was uncomfortable, you would undress yourself too, as a gesture of respect. You would look at my bare body, each and every line, every single curve, and draw it, layer it with paint and bring it alive. Your eyes focused on the canvas while mine focused on you, your brown eyes only aware of the lines and colours, your curly hair sitting on your head in a rough mop, your broad muscular shoulders, your chest with the patches of light hair that promised a thick cover with age. But you never aged.

They say love is all there is in this huge, wide world. Love is what helps you pass through heaven's door. Love is what can melt the hardest stones, it is what brings many to the right path. I had found such love in you, Arun, how can I ever let it go?

Arun has returned. He comes to see me. I am no longer as miserable as I was before. He tells me what I should do, how I should deal with my problems. At times we talk and at times he just sits next to me, keeps looking at me lovingly. No matter what he does when he is here, his presence always makes me happy.

I found a box under my bed this morning. I thought I had misplaced it a long time ago. I was so delighted to find it again. It had so many things I thought I had lost forever. That little sketch you had made for me when Sunaina's mean little postcard had made me cry. The box even had that postcard. But now the box has disappeared again. I know I placed it on the table when I found it and it is not there any more. Maybe Arun took it when he left. Maybe he had brought it when he came to see me last night. Maybe it had been with him all these years. It's okay. I don't need to worry. He would bring it back. I am reading a book he had once gifted me. It's a collection of translations of Rumi's poetry. I remember reading this book with Arun at his apartment. He would sit on the little red Kashmiri carpet he had brought from Srinagar two years ago. 'It's God's paradise destroyed by man.' That was all he said when I had asked him about Kashmir. I loved the carpet. I was fascinated by those colourful lines which twisted and turned and wove themselves together into stars, octagons, hexagons to create intricate geometric patterns in indigo, white, red and shades of green. I used to call it the magic carpet. He would sit there, in the corner of the living room, resting his back against the wall. I would lay my head on his lap and read to him. Together we would fly off to faraway places, secure and safe, birthed by our imagination. I had read out many parts of this book to him, again, and again as he gently stroked my hair. This book was his favourite.

I feel a tingle in my right ear. I smile. I know he is here. I turn around. He is standing there. Loving smile on his face. I get up.

'I got something for you,' he says. He has the magic carpet rolled under his arm. He spreads it in the corner of the room. He sits there and looks at me. I sit down next to him. I rest my head on his lap. He strokes my hair. Moments of comforting silence pass. After a while I begin to feel uneasy. I am sad for no reason. My vision is blurred by a veil of tears. Arun continues to stroke my hair tenderly. The silence in the room is broken by his gentle, soothing voice. 'You have to stop living in the past. You must know that time gone by will never come back. The memories only make you sad.' I lie there, listening to him, holding my breath. I want him to keep talking forever, to be here forever. 'And you should not hope for a better tomorrow. It's the way of a lazy dreamer who does nothing but hope. Learn to live in the moment. Enjoy the present. Only that can make you happy.'

'But how? How should I do that?'

'You are holding on to me too tight, Maya. You need to learn to let go.'

I get up and look into his eyes. What is he saying? Why is he saying this?

'Just look around. Look at your room. You have stored a part of me in everything around you. These framed pictures on the walls, these books on your study table, this whole almirah full of the gifts I gave you.'

'But these are things that you gave me. You gave them to me with love.'

'And now these things are causing you pain,' he says, his eyes firm on me.

'My love is a part of you, Maya. I have planted it deep inside your heart just like you have planted yours deep inside mine. And it will always remain there. No one can ever take it away from you or from me. You must not feel insecure about it.'

I look down at the carpet. The complex colourful lines baffle me. 'What should I do?' I ask.

'Pack all this stuff and give it away,' he says as easily as he breathes.

I shake my head.

'You have to do this for me. Promise me.'

I stare back at him, frozen with the pain of the words I have just heard. I can't even bear to hear them. How would I ever be able to go through with it? He sits there smiling at me. I try to smile but fail.

'Let's talk about something else. What is up these days? What's new?' he asks.

'Mom wanted me to resume my studies. I have started going to college again,' I say. I can't look him in the eyes right now. I have managed to hold back my tears, I don't want to break down now.

'Well, that's great! How is that going?'

'It's not that easy, Arun. I have to repeat the whole year. Everyone around me is new. All the people I knew are in second year now. There is no one I know. And . . .'

'And what?'

I struggle to gather my words and say, 'You are not there.'

'I am there, Maya. I will always be there with you. Whenever you want me. And about your friends, you will make new ones. You've got to be brave, Maya. One cannot live like this.'

I don't like what he is saying. It's the first time that I don't like the words that come out of his lips. The lips that have rained so many loving kisses on me. The lips that have confessed his love countless times to me.

20

Garun

Anything for the riches, even sex with an old hag!

I don't normally indulge in small talk. The moment I enter the room with my 'client' I get down to business. I have already stripped, and I am waiting for her to come out of the washroom. Man, she is taking a long time. Finally she emerges in lacy lingerie. God, I hate it when these old sluts think they look hot. She lies down next to me and I give her a small smile. Her wrinkly boobs are really not something I want to look at. So I delay the 'stripping her' part. I put my legs around her and sit on top of her. I touch her all over and start licking her neck, then I smooch her for a long time. I start massaging her breasts and slowly move in a way that my dick rubs on her lacy panties. The foreplay with these oldies really takes a while. But whatever . . . anything for the money. I then get off the bed and turn off the lights to save myself the torture of looking at her sagging, fat body. I keep my condom ready on the side table along with a small bottle of baby oil for lubrication. I climb on top of her again and strip her completely. I run my hands all over her and move down to her thighs. I tease her a bit and then move my hand in her pussy. She is a little wet. Not enough though. I go to the washroom and get a towel dipped in warm water. I spread her legs apart and wipe her vagina with the towel. She is just lying there. Unamused. I will show this bitch what I can do. I use my hands and open the lips of her pussy. I massage it a bit and then I start licking her with my tongue. I do it gently at first and she is already getting excited. I lick her even deeper, and moving my hands to her ass, I squeeze it. She is moaning now and I am ready to fuck her. A few more seconds and she is all wet and ready to be fucked. I move up and position myself to put my dick in her. I quickly wear my condom and lubricate it with the oil. I enter her and start moving. She grabs my ass and digs in her nails. It arouses me. She moans and I thrust even harder. I can see her saggy boobs jumping up and down in the dim light of the room. I bend down and almost hug her to make her body stop moving. Her hands are all over my back. I move faster and she is almost breathless. Good. She is about to come.

I go to the washroom, masturbate and clean up. These women always climax before me. I go out to find her still naked on the bed. I start putting on my clothes when she says, 'I want to do it again.'

'It will cost double the amount we settled for,' I say. I am not a charity service after all.

'Sure.' She smiles.

'I need a fifteen-minute break,' I say as I sit on the sofa and swipe through my phone. She is in the washroom now. In less than fifteen minutes I am ready to go again. When she returns I am waiting on the bed with the condom and everything ready on the side.

'I want to be on top this time,' she says.

What the fuck? But I hide my reaction and simply smile. 'Come on, that's not a good idea. I am here to take care of you and you should just relax and enjoy.' Come on! Who wants to take her weight? It will be exhausting. But she is not convinced. 'Or we can do something else,' I say. 'We can go for a sixty-nine instead.'

She looks at me for a while and finally nods. Good. At least I will get sucked too this time. She lies down and I climb on top with my head towards her vagina. I spread her legs and she starts massaging my dick. It's so much better now that I cannot see her old wrinkly face and boobs. I massage her pussy with my fingers first and then I start licking her. I get charged up as she puts my dick in her mouth and sucks me like a lollipop. I lick her pussy hard and deep. She moans as she sucks me. She is completely wet and I am about to cum. I warn her but she continues to suck. I cum in her mouth and she swallows. I bite her pussy and I finger her till she climaxes. We are done. If she asks me again, I am going to charge her triple.

21

Maya

Wrapped in a comfortable nakedness with Arun

I set my phone and Bluetooth speakers on the ledge where I know the splashes of water will not reach when I take my shower. I put on my favourite song, 'Dast-e-tanhai'. The alaap starts. The song is magical. It calms my nerves like nothing else. It somehow consoles me, tells me everything is all right, that I am not alone in feeling the way I do. I undress and hang my clothes on the hooks on the closed brown bathroom door. I like the feel of the cold white bathroom tiles under my feet. I grasp the cold, shiny chrome-plated shower knob and turn it. Water gushes down on me as I adjust the temperature. I like my shower hotter than most people might. I like the feel of the hot water on my skin. I like how it first feels like I may have burnt my skin but then the water only comforts my senses.

I like being in the shower. This is the only place where I can be myself. This is the only place where I don't need to wear a mask, or a robe to hide myself. I don't need to worry that someone is watching me, thinking about me, forming an opinion and deciding how to talk to me or how to treat me.

Steam fills the bathroom. It is so thick that I can barely see the door, which is now a mere haze behind the cloud of steam. I close my eyes and let the hot water run down my body. It is making me feel alive. As if the hot water has collected all the pieces of my body that had broken off, drifted far away from me, from each other. It has pulled them all together, joining them with a fresh new skin that holds them tight. I feel new.

I open my eyes and stare at the hazy brown door. Soon it starts to change colour to a lighter shade of brown and then to the colour of skin. The skin of someone I know, the skin of someone I love. It moves forward. A face appears. He is here. Arun is here. I look at him and smile. He smiles back. He stands there with me in the shower as we silently look into each other's eyes. I hug him. He hugs me back. I kiss him. He kisses me back.

He picks up the soap and gently starts lathering it over my shoulders. I close my eyes. I want to lose myself in the moment.

I don't know how long we stand there. It is his voice that brings me back from my trance. 'How is it going? How do you like going to college again?'

He wants me to go on with my life and I cannot tell him I do not like going to college. I don't want to upset him – I can't afford to. 'I would have liked it better if you were there with me too,' I finally say.

'If I go there with you, you won't make new friends.'

I hug him. I hold him tighter than I ever have before. 'Why can't you come back? Why can't you come back to my life?' I want to cry my eyes out. I want to howl, the heartache is unbearable.

'Things are going to be fine, Maya. In time, everything will be fine.' He strokes my head, my wet hair clinging to my skin. We look into each other's eyes. I kiss his shoulder, his neck, his face, his eyes. I rain kisses all over him, kisses of love, of passion. But he just stands there with his arms around me. I see no passion in him. I feel no passion in him. I let go and take a step back. He steps forward, holds up my hair and massages the back of my neck.

'I want you to have a good life, Maya. That's all I want for you. You had forgotten this. That is why I had to come back.'

Suddenly the water from the shower is hurting me. It is pricking my skin like sharp needles, wounding every inch of my body. There is blood all over me. I am bathed in my own blood. There are streams of blood on the white floor, flowing into the drain. My gaze darts towards Arun in panic but he simply shakes his head. I look at my body again, at my hands and my feet. I run my hands on my belly and chest. The blood is gone. Only water. I hug Arun again and he holds me tight. 'It's all right. Everything is fine. I am never going to leave you.'

And that is all I need to hear. That is all I need.

22

Garun

Because nothing sells like hot, naked sex

Across cultures, across time and across ages, sex has always been the best, the most sure-shot and foolproof way to make money, something that never fails. Something that can never go wrong. I just finished fucking a woman. And she is kind of funny. We are done with everything but she wants me to remain naked as long as we are in the room. She is sitting on the sofa, smoking a cigarette, completely naked. Her gaze follows me as I walk around the room. After I did her I went for a shower, came out drying myself and asked her, 'So, what next?'

'Nothing,' she said, smiling at me, her loose boobs hanging on her chest and her fat hips sitting on the sofa.

She is the kind who looks decent only when dressed, a disgrace when naked.

'Shall we leave, then?' I ask.

'No, let's just be here for a while.'

We don't really have anything to talk about. I keep things discreet and professional. I fuck my clients and let them go. No questions whatsoever. I don't ask who they are, what they do or where they are from. I don't even ask their name. If you really want to know, I don't really give a shit about them. I don't even care if it's a man or a woman. A pussy or an ass, how does it make a difference? A hole is a hole. And the tighter it is, the better. As long as they give me the money, it's all cool. I have fucked over twenty-one women and six men. At times I have to fuck more than one person a day. The business is going well. My bank balance has gone up by over three hundred thousand rupees since I started and it's fucking awesome!

I walk to the window and look outside. It's a busy night like every other. Cars lined up on the road. Their headlights like small beads of liquid gold, strung together as if they were a complex, dynamic, tangled necklace the city was wearing tonight.

My life has changed. The tables have turned. Nowadays women pick me up from wherever I ask them to. Generally they send a chauffeur-driven car – an Audi, BMW or a Mercedes, at least. We have dinner at a fine-dining restaurant and then the old hag takes me to the hotel room. And these bitches are rich! Most of them married to rich, powerful industrialists. They never think below seven star. They even drop me wherever I want to be dropped. Oh man, I love this. Who says making money is tough. It hasn't even been a month since I got my website up and I haven't spent a single weekend alone.

I can feel the old woman's gaze on my back. She can look at my Greek-god-like body and get all the thrills she wants. I know she is getting wet sitting there on the sofa, just by looking at me. That's how I am – the best at whatever I do, be it sex or anything else.

23

Sasha

The hunting game

Sasha's husband is back from another trip to Europe with no travel plans for the next week or so. She cannot go out clubbing, or for drinks to the bars – her favourite hunting grounds. She must resort to what she finds the most boring way to hunt. She will have to find someone online.

She turns her laptop on, puts it on the bed and walks over to the door to make sure her husband is still working in the study. He must be going through those endless and complex spreadsheets, and won't get up for hours. She goes on to Google and types 'hot sexy male escort'. The screen pulls up a long list of links. She has used and exhausted all the men listed on the first few pages of the search. It's only on the fourth page that she finds a fresh body. The website claims that the guy provides a 'fucking good service'. There are pictures of the 'service provider' there as well. A young well-toned, muscular male body – a good specimen. Tempting. Well cut. Broad chest and a narrow waist. Defined six-pack abs. There are around five pictures taken from different angles. In all of them he is wearing a Batman mask and tight black briefs, lining his genitals. Sasha wants to whip that body bloody already, she wants to dig her nails deep and tear his skin.

There is a button on the page that says 'Get in touch to get fucked'. She clicks on it and a message window opens. She knows what she wants to say to this hot-bod.

> Hello Lovah!
> I love your body, you sex god! And I want you to fuck me hard with your rock-hard dick. And I want a lot more of you. But I will explain that when we meet. In this meeting, I promise, there would be no fucking. There will be no stroking. There won't even be any touching. I will give you twenty thousand only to meet me once and get naked in front of me. I will tell you what I want from you apart from your fucking service. You can take up my offer or you can turn it down. If you are *up* for this, let me know. I will tell you where to come. We will meet privately.

Such matters can't be discussed in pubic places. Oops! I meant public places ;)

Love and sex

Your mystery lovah

Sasha looks at her message and smiles. The honey trap has been set. It is the time of year when she takes one special prey far away to her summer home. And she has just found the right candidate for it.

~

Garun reads the message twice. An incredible twenty thousand only to get naked in front of someone in private and talk! He never knew earning money was this easy. And this woman sounds hot. He can sense she is naughty and dirty in bed. Oh, how he loves that. He is getting a hard-on just thinking how things might go. Immediately he types the reply –

Where do I have to cum? Oops! Sorry, I meant come ;)

Love and fuck

Your hottest sex god ever

24

Sasha

Body inspection

Sasha gets a call from the reception.

'Good evening ma'am, there is a gentleman here to meet you.'

'Yes, please direct him to my room.'

In less than two minutes there is a knock on the door. 'Come in,' she calls and seats herself on the sofa by the window. The door opens and a young man strides into the room, so confident as if he owns it. He stops when he notices the woman sitting in front of him. He smiles. She is a treat to his eyes, long slender legs, firm round breasts, flawless olive skin. Her body is covered in a sheer, see-through robe as light as the air around her.

Eight massive diamond rings adorn her fingers. She is rich. He must milk her well.

'Welcome,' Sasha says as she walks up to him, giving him a quick scan. He is dressed in blue jeans and a loose red T-shirt that falls on his lean, muscular frame accentuating his shoulders and chest. His dark brown hair is messy in a charming way. Light stubble on the jaw that will take a few years to thicken up – the sign of a man stepping out of boyhood into manhood.

They stand in front of each other. They smile. Both like what they see. 'I am glad I stumbled upon your website.' Sasha breaks the silence.

'I am glad you found it too,' the young man responds with a cocky grin.

'I know what you look like. I know what the best part of your body is. But I don't know your name,' Sasha hisses. Her gaze pinning him like a lioness observing her prey.

'I can say the same for you,' the boy says. 'I know your boobs are the best I have ever seen. I want to cup and lick them right here, right now, but I don't know your name.'

'If you understand the arrangement, I am the one who sets the rules. I am the one who pays the money. I am the one who is to be obeyed.'

He looks at Sasha mutely.

'Don't worry, I am not one of those cheap sluts who will run after you when you are done. I won't call you and message you hundred times a day and accuse you of playing with me. When I am done with a man, I never see his face again.'

After a pause the boy says, 'Garun.'

'Nice to meet you, Garun. I think it would be wonderful to fuck you. My name is Sasha, by the way.'

'Thanks, I think it would be wonderful to fuck you too.' Garun smiles smugly.

'So . . .' She turns around and paces back to the sofa and sits down. 'A young man hungry for money. Here to meet a woman who is almost double his age. You must be in a real hurry to build up your fortune.'

'Yes, this world runs on money and fame. And anonymity is worse than death these days. I want to be rich and famous, and I will do anything for it.'

Something in his voice tells Sasha that he is not sharing his feelings or pouring his heart out to his new-found friend. He is only indicating that his service can't be bought cheap. Sasha smiles again. She likes it when men play games with her. Poor things, they always underestimate her. They think she is a woman, weaker than them. They can snub her, manipulate her and play with her the way they want. The whole idea makes her want to throw her head back and laugh. She shifts a little to get more comfortable. She feels like a powerful queen sitting on a throne, who can control any man and yet has nothing to hide from anybody.

'Your peace of mind – that's the price you have to pay for fame.' With her eyes fixed on Garun, Sasha takes a pause to make sure her words echo in his mind. 'Come on now, take off your clothes,' she says, looking fiercely into his eyes. 'Or do you want me to do it for you? Like a mother does for her three-year-old child? Come on now, get naked.'

Garun pulls off his T-shirt, puts his hands on his waist and grins, putting himself confidently on display.

'Scared to take off the rest of your clothes? Something you want to conceal?'

Garun takes off his shoes and socks. He unbuttons and unzips his jeans. Dropping them along with his briefs on the floor, he steps out of them as he lightly juggles his dick with his hands to make sure it gets a rush of blood and does not look shrunken. He puts his hands on his waist again and grins back at her. 'How do you like me now?' he asks.

'A nice package.' She stands up. 'Please turn around.'

Garun turns around, flexing and flinching his butt as Sasha inspects him silently. She moves closer to him and runs a finger lightly up his back. Her touch is electrifying. It sends waves of excitement over Garun's body.

'Turn around,' she says again.

Garun is already semi-erect. She puts her finger on his chest, barely touching it. His skin was sprouting thin, light hair over his sternum. A few strands around the nipples. She can feel the pounding of his heart against his chest. She steps closer. She can even hear it faintly in the quiet of the room.

'Our existence is held in boundaries and those boundaries are our bodies. The touch of someone else's skin, I find, is something very astounding.' She runs her finger down his chest deliberately grazing his nipple, down to his abs. 'My skin against someone else's . . . that's where I end and the other starts. That's when I actually feel them.' She slides her hand further down. 'I actually know who they are, what they are like. Like right now I feel you.' Sasha grabs Garun's balls, the unexpected move making his body jolt. 'Right now, I know all of you, only you,' she hisses like a snake. And then she releases Garun as unexpectedly as she had grabbed him.

She walks away from him and stands next to the window. The city is waking up for the night. People are lighting up their houses to drive away the darkness that is building up after the sun has set, the night is growing stronger. 'You don't need to do anything more today,' she says, with a smooth, swift turn that makes her light chiffon robe flare around her as if it just breathed heavily. 'You will get forty thousand for today as I touched you. I know you were not expecting it. Now listen to my offer very carefully. I will subject you to something that you have never experienced before. I will take you to a special place, far away from the city. You will stay there with me for a week. I will have sex with you every day. And every day I will notch things up a little. I will subject you to things that you have never dreamt of. Nor will you ever experience those things again in your life. I will bind you, entice you, seduce you, then I will edge you, you will beg to cum and I will tease you more, push you to your limits. We will see how much of a man you are.' Garun can see Sasha's nipples harden as she speaks. 'And for this, I will pay you fifty lakh rupees.'

Garun looks at her in silent agreement. He already has a rock-hard erection. Money, sex and power. Things could not get more enticing than this. He can hardly wait.

25

Maya

Her distorted reality

Mom cried today. She broke down in front of me. We all cry alone, we all have those private moments when we hide ourselves in the bathroom and weep our hearts out making sure that we don't make a sound – making sure no one gets to know. But when we cry in front of someone, it's almost like a plea for help, a desperate, frantic call. Mom said it kills her to see me this way. That's all she said, again and again. Then she broke into a fit of sobs. I remember she told me once that no other bond can be as strong as that of a mother and her child. Then why does she not understand that I am happy. I am happier than I was before. Arun makes sure of that. The other day he brought a beautiful gift for me. Something unlike I had ever seen before. It was a transparent potted plant. It has beautiful long leaves that curl slightly towards the ends. It has a definite structure of growth – each stem sprouts a ring of six buds at regular intervals. But if you look at it as a whole, it is a chaotic bush. It is really a magical plant. He said this plant is just like life – you can make it look like anything you want. And that's actually true. The transparent leaves, stems and flowers – I just have to look at them and think what colour I want them to be and they turn into that colour. From a small bush, it has grown into a huge plant that now spreads out in the whole room. But it does not really bother me. It just makes my room a lot more beautiful.

I walk to the mirror on the wall, careful not to step on any of the branches on the floor. I look at my reflection with the beautiful magical plant all around me in the background, throwing beams of colourful light as though passing through a glass prism. My mother says she understands me like no one else, she wants to see me happy. Why can't she see I *am* happy?

Slowly the image in the mirror starts to change. Slowly the clothes I am wearing start to dissolve in the air around me. The fabric thins and disappears completely. I am naked. I stand there staring at myself. Frozen. A gas starts to ooze out of my navel, a light brown gas. It forms a cloud. It grows into a long, linear cloud that extends from my navel to an arm's distance.

The end of the cloud starts to grow into a bulb. It expands as the long cloud becomes narrower, like a rope. It becomes dense. The bulb at the end takes the shape of a fetus, floating lightly in the air, right next to the mirror. It grows into a small infant and then a boy. The face is familiar. The shoulders grow broader. The legs grow long. The muscles grow thick. His eyes are open and fixed on me. His hairline changes, defining his sideburns. A light moustache appears, then his beard. Finally the chord connecting my navel to him dissolves into the air, just like my clothes. We stand there looking at each other. Naked. We have nothing to hide from each other. He holds my hand and takes me to the bed. We walk in the room with the magnificent, glimmering plant all around us. It looks like heaven.

We sit on the bed. Everything around us is radiating with peace and pleasure.

'How is your new life?' he asks me.

'It is nice. I like it.' I smile.

'I am very happy to hear that.'

'Did you make any new friends?'

'Not really.'

'You should try.'

'I don't know . . . it's nice to go out of the house once again, have a regular routine. I understand the subjects better now. I actually get the meaning of so many ideas and philosophies that I did not get at all when I was studying them before.'

I fall silent. He asks me something. I try to avoid his question but I really can't. He is looking at me. He is smiling. It's a smile that understands my struggles. A smile that is sympathetic. A smile that is soothing.

'I tried to make friends, Arun. I tried. But it's . . . it's not easy. Everyone looks at me with such judgemental eyes. As if I am a girl who has lost her mind . . . a girl plagued with a dangerous disease who would infect them if they came too close. I can almost hear them, their strange stories. Stories made up for the sole purpose of entertainment. Stories about me – the crazy girl with a twisted mind, Arun. But I am not that. *I am not that*!'

Arun listens to me patiently. He wants to know more.

'But there is this one boy. He came to talk to me.' Arun nods and tells me to go on.

'He was trying to be extra nice to me. It was a little strange. You know how I feel about people who are too nice to me. I didn't talk to him. I didn't respond.'

'You are strange, Maya.' Arun flashes me the same radiant smile he used to have every evening we met. The smile that said 'you are my crazy little girl, when will you ever learn'. 'You are saying that all of them look at you like you are crazy and the one who does want to talk to you, you find him suspicious.'

He does not understand. I could see the boy's intentions. It was not just friendship that he wanted. Arun holds me by the shoulders. A soft, firm, warm, loving grip. 'Trust someone once again, Maya. Give him a chance.'

'I don't know . . . it feels strange when he is around . . . he is nothing like me. He is so different . . . his tastes, his likes . . . we have nothing in common at all. How can we ever be friends?' I don't know how to explain it further.

'Yes, he is very different and that's exactly the reason he would be able to help you. If both of you were the same, both of you thought similarly, he would never be able to find a solution to your problems, he would never be able to help you.'

Silence

'Give him a chance,' he repeats.

Part 2

Don’t ask, don’t tell!

26

Sasha

That brutal artist

Sasha did not tell him where they were going. All Garun knew was that they were headed to an isolated place somewhere deep in the mountains. They left the busy city in her private airplane. When they landed on her private airstrip, there was not a man in sight. The place was not silent as one might call it – it was echoing with the sounds of nature. The wind was howling, like a gigantic monster whizzing around, hunting for prey. The bamboo leaves were rustling, playing a strange music of their own and a distant stream, nowhere in sight, was sending out a calming hum of running water. They had landed right in the centre of a valley – low mountains behind them, and huge, snow-covered, higher ones in front.

There is a jeep parked under a shed. Sasha purposefully walks over to the jeep, pulling a key out of her bag. She knows she does not have to direct him, she knows Garun is following her. She knows she is in control. It is a ten-minute drive to the mansion. After silently driving for a while on the narrow metalled road flanked with thin vegetation along its edges, Sasha says, 'We are at a height of 3200 metres. This is covered in ten feet thick snow for the major part of the year. I always come here for a couple of weeks every summer. I love this place.' She turns to him and adds, 'And every year, I bring along a different companion with me.'

'You own this land?' Garun asks. Sasha can smell a hint of intimidation in his voice. She smiles. Finally the truth has crept under his skin, finally he has understood how powerful she is.

'Yes, this is my property.'

'How much of it? I mean . . . that little airport, is that yours too?'

'It is.'

Silence.

'As far as your eyes can see right now, I am the queen of all you survey.'

'Impressive.'

It is an expansive property, so vast that even if you screamed and yelled at the top of your lungs, no one would ever hear you.

The mansion is unlike anything he could have imagined – it is grander than his imagination. As they enter, they step into a triple-height gallery which can easily hold at least a hundred people. It is evident from Garun's walk that he feels small. At a glance, the space looks empty and simple but it doesn't take long for one to realize that the huge wooden panels, intricately carved, hugging the walls, going up at least fifteen feet are actually leafed with gold. The massive chandelier hanging in the centre has huge jewels embedded and hanging from it.

'Those are artificial diamonds, what they call cubic zirconia, along with some jades and sapphires. I sourced some of those stones from an antiques dealer in Portugal. He said they date back to the sixteenth century, and were traded sometime later from a Konkan king in the eighteenth century. He had a special map tracing the history of those pieces along with various family trees of all the people who ever owned them. But I never cared for any of that – the history and the significance. Stones are stones, some look good and some don't, it's as simple as that. And if I really think about it, why is it so important what happened to these stones in the last six hundred years or so? They were formed way before that, isn't it? The connections of such objects with humans, with civilizations, I find, are very trivial. The earth is way older than human existence.'

Garun remains fixed to his spot, staring at the huge chandelier. It is hanging high above him but it still looks as massive as an elephant. How much would it be worth?

Sasha is deriving pleasure from Garun's bewilderment. She leaves him in this state of awe for a while and then says, 'Come, I will show you the gallery.'

The door that opens to the left is grander than the one at the entrance lobby. The room is windowless with a huge circular skylight in the ceiling.

'This room is a discrete cube, sides forty feet each. I wanted the idea of the four elements of nature to echo in here, where I displayed my art. After all, art comes from nature. The circle that you see above, from where the light falls in during the day and darkness during the night, is a reminder of the only absolute truth of the cosmos – the cycle of infinity.'

The paintings on the walls are larger than any Garun had ever seen, each at least fifteen feet tall.

'If you know how to read a painting, I would like you to look at them from a distance first, as a whole, go closer, look at the different parts of it and then go even closer and see the details, the true expression. That's how you experience the emotion that it truly conveys.'

The paintings have a very distinct style. The massive use of the colour red ties them all together. Most of them are violent scenes with fountains of blood and fire – either a woman tearing up the entrails of a man or a man tearing up the entrails of a woman. Some have godlike, beautiful faces. The actions they perform are extremely brutal, but a divine peace radiates from their faces, as if they are entranced by some soulful music or enraptured by the beauty of nature. The paintings are powerful. If you listen closely you can almost hear screams and yells emanating from them. One of the paintings shows a nine foot tall cat pawing a lizard around three feet long. Garun is looking at it intently when Sasha comes and stands right beside him. As he turns away from the painting to move on to the next one, she steps in his way. 'Have you ever seen a cat kill its prey? Making it believe that it could escape and live on, right till the last moment, until it has slowly squeezed the life out of it. I find it very profound, poetic and beautiful in its own way.'

'I don't know why they do it,' she goes on. 'It's really intriguing. Some day I want to find out what doing that feels like.'

Garun looks into her eyes for a while before he says, 'You are a very dangerous person.' A smile slowly creeps on Sashas's face because she hears more than what the boy has said. His words said that she was dangerous but his eyes said that he was not scared of her. She likes it, she likes his courage. She finds it enticing.

'Everyone is dangerous, Garun, even you are. After all, we are humans.' Sasha's strong gaze has Garun rooted in his place.

'Your work is really good,' Garun says as she finally loosens her invisible grip on him and he moves on to the next painting. 'Why don't you sell them? I am sure they would bring in big money.'

'If you do something to earn money, you earn only money and nothing else. You never really achieve anything or any growth in your skill and art.'

'But all this . . . great work, this great art, it should be recognized, acknowledged. Seriously, it's better than a lot of award-winning stuff that I have seen.'

Sasha smiles again. 'All awards are strongly PR driven activities. None of them are genuine, no matter how big or small, they are all fake.' She pauses and looks at him again with a smile even more mysterious. 'But that does not mean if I get one tomorrow, I won't accept it.'

They move in silence from one painting to another before they reach a portrait of a woman. This piece is different from the rest because of its colours but the emotion it portrays is just as grave. In the background there are multiple rainbows being engulfed by leaping walls of fire and the huge waves of a red sea of blood. Stabbed, bloody unicorns falling into pits of fire that were supposed to be the rainbows' ends. The woman in the foreground weeps silently, her tears crystallized into perfect ice cubes as they roll down her cheeks. Cubes as perfect as the room they are in. Garun can understand. It is a self-portrait. Her misery is oozing out of her art as well.

'Is it true what they say?' Garun asks turning to her. 'Is it true that good art comes from misery? Out of a shattered, broken heart?'

Sasha seems lost in thought, caught in an old memory.

'Have you ever wept so much, for so long, that your tears turn cold on your face? That's when you know you are unhappy, that you are miserable. And you need to do something about it. I am miserable.' She looks at him again, alert and aware this time. 'I know. But that's not the sad part. The sad part is that I know why I am sad and I can do nothing about it.

'We live in a world where our own shadows that follow us are always darker and bigger than us. Our past haunts us in ways that we don't even understand at times.'

'But you are channelling it so well. A broken heart sings the sweetest songs, they say. Your paintings are beautiful.'

'The perception of the emotion of love changes with age. Ask yourself "what is love" after every ten years and your answer will be different each time.'

'You are young. You must be in love.'

'Me? No!' Garun retorts. 'No one can understand me enough to love me. And I would never love anyone if they don't love me back.'

Sasha sees something unexpected in Garun's eyes. It is a flash of self-loathing. Is she imagining it? Is her mind making her see what she wants to or is she misinterpreting his ego? 'I read this somewhere and it made a lot of sense – not everyone is going to like you, no matter how nice, how good you are. And not everyone is going to hate you, no matter how bad, how evil you are.'

She has Garun's attention. She can see it in his eyes that he wants her to tell him more. 'But then, it's also true that no one loves you for who you really are as a whole. People only love you because they want a part of you, the part they find pleasing. It upsets them if they see the part of you that they don't like, they don't approve of. They only want that reflection of their own thoughts because they want to satisfy their own self, and this self-gratification they call love. They want you around only because they want *you* to love them and care for them. It's all imbalanced.' She meets his eyes and says, 'No one ever loves you the way they say they do.'

She pulls out a cigarette from her bag, lights it, takes a deep drag, and blows it out slowly and a little cloud starts to float in front of her face, cutting Garun's clear vision. She walks out of the gallery to the next room as

Garun follows her silently. She sits down on a sofa and gestures to Garun to sit in front of her.

'Love is a crazy thing,' she says. 'I read a story about one such love, once. A man and a woman, they loved each other more than anyone can love another. The husband died in an accident. The wife hugged the body and wept and howled for days. She could not really accept that her husband was dead, could not come to terms with the concept of mortality. She wanted to defy the gods, defy nature itself. She did not want to part with him, ever. But she knew if she kept his body with herself, he would rot and eventually vanish. She wanted him to be a part of her forever. So she decided to eat him instead of cremating him. And that's how he became a part of her forever. After she digested him, parts of his body became a part of her own body.' She ashed her cigarette in the ashtray. 'What was the name of the author again? . . . Why can't I recall . . . something with R . . .' she says, wracking her mind, frowning.

'Rohit Sehdev,' Garun offers.

'Yes! I like his writing. Makes a lot of sense. He says things you can actually follow in life.' Sasha snaps her fingers. She looks at Garun as he looks down at the floor with unseeing eyes. She does not interrupt him. She lets his thoughts churn in his mind.

He finally looks up at her and says, 'You know so

much, why don't you teach? You can encourage some great artists.'

Sasha takes another drag from her cigarette and says, 'You can't really teach anything to anyone. People learn things on their own. That's why I think teaching is a wasteful profession.'

Garun's eyes light up with satisfaction at this.

'You know why we are here?' she asks him.

'To have sex,' Garun says, matter-of-factly.

'You know I am married and have children?'

'No, I didn't. I could have guessed it but . . . it does not matter.'

'You know what we are about to do is looked upon as a sin by the world?'

'Yeah.'

'But you will still do it?'

'Yes.'

'Why?

'For money. And also because I don't care about such things.' He shrugs.

'You know I will bind you. I will hurt you too.'

'Now I know.' There is no hesitation or fear in Garun's voice.

'It's funny we just talked about that writer because in some ways it was one of his books, I think, that changed the way I think. When I stepped out of the boundaries of my marriage for the first time, I was full of doubts. I was anxious not only about my actions being considered a sin but also because I was inflicting a lot of pain on other men. But then, while it was happening, while I was in the middle of it all, I asked myself how I felt. And that was my moment of realization. I had no doubt about it – I felt *good*. I had never felt so right doing something so wrong.' She flicks the ash off her cigarette. 'And then I thought, if something felt so good, instinctively, naturally, it had to be right. It had to be natural and *it had to be*,' she says, clenching her fist, narrowing her eyes. 'I was meant to do it. That whole realization happened in an instant, a flash, like a strike of lightning it opened my eyes with a jolt. And after that, I never looked back. Today, it's like a service I do for a larger purpose, it's what I am meant to do.'

Silence.

'You are young, Garun. This is going to scar you. But that's nothing to worry about. It's not the scars that trouble you in life. It's how you treat your scars that determines how they affect your life,' she says and then looks away. She is not sure how she has treated her own scars, if they still hurt and trouble her.

27

Sasha

Love in the mountains?

'It's always your dreams and your realities that play the duet of your life,' Sasha says. 'You said you were doing this for the money and money is what you are going to get. Your dream is on its way to becoming a reality. I can almost hear the song of your life. I can see it till the very end. Desire is what you want the most but experience the least. But you will attain some of your desires.'

She comes closer to Garun and smiles as they both stand in front of each other. Garun is naked as a baby and Sasha is dressed in a red chiffon robe. The night is a lot colder than the day, even more than expected. Outside, a thick mist is wrapping itself around the huge mansion, intending to hide it from plain sight. Inside, the room is dimly lit. A fire crackles and flickers, their shadows quivering and shaking on the wall. All the muscles in Garun's body are tight. His skin is erupting into goose-flesh, partly from excitement and partly from the cold. His breath forms tiny clouds of mist when he exhales. Sasha tilts her head, leans forward and sucks in one such cloud of his breath.

'What is mist but cold vapour in the air? What is fire, but awfully hot, shimmering air? Even something as invisible as air glows, becomes visible and can even hurt if you subject it to extremes. We are only human, we can become more dangerous if we are disturbed,' Sasha says, caressing his chest. Garun is beginning to get hard.

Two thick chains hang from the ceiling with leather straps at their ends. Sasha lifts Garun's left arm and straps his wrist, while his right arm remains loose.

'They say violent desires have violent ends. All of this might bring my doom some day but I can't help it.' She pauses and looks right into his eyes and says, 'I love this so much.'

After some moments of silence she asks, gently stroking his dick, 'What will you prefer first, the whip, the kick or the electricity?'

'The electricity.'

Sasha smiles. 'Good choice. Now the rule of the game is that you cannot move your right hand. No matter how hard it hurts.' She is so close to him that she can feel his warm breath on her skin. 'You cannot use it to stop me, to stop the pain.' She rubs her thigh against his thigh, her belly against his belly, her breasts against his chest and her pelvis against his pelvis. 'Understood?'

'Yes.'

'Good.' She walks to the wall on which numerous instruments are hung. They have been systematically arranged. The top row is whips. The second row is electric stunners. The third row is straps, dildos and balls of different sizes. She notices Garun's head is turned towards the wall, and he is observing what all it has to offer.

'I call it the wall of pain. It has all my favourite toys. And this wall is going to give you an experience of a lifetime.'

Sasha stands in front of the wall for a while. All the instruments have handles the same size but their shafts vary in size and form. One has a broad metal comb that would send multiple electrical impulses to the body. There's one with a round glass bulb at its end, then there's a single metal shaft that would give out a little blue spark when flicked against the skin. One has two pointed needles placed two inches or so apart, between which an electric current would run. This is her favourite – she loves to use it on erect dicks and useless man nipples. She takes it off the hook and walks back to Garun.

'You know, we are nothing without electricity,' she says, standing in front of him. 'Our brain' – she runs a finger down his head – 'sends these tiny electrical impulses' – down his neck, his ripped shoulders, his chest – 'to various parts of our body' – over his flexed, washboard abs – 'and directs them what to do.' She grabs his balls tight and tugs them hard. Garun does not flinch. He seems to be prepared for this. As soon as she releases his balls, his dick rapidly turns fully erect and hard.

'Woah! I like that.' She winks at him. 'Now brace yourself. This is where the fun begins.'

She flicks his left nipple to start things off. His whole body shakes. He clenches his teeth. She smiles. She flicks his nipple again. His body shakes again. His lips pursed, he shuts his eyes tight and opens them. She flicks the same nipple again. Taking a deep breath, he clenches his fist but does not move his arm. Sasha smiles as she flicks the same nipple again. A tiny trail of smoke snakes up in the air. Some hair around the nipple has burnt. There is a tiny, dark burn mark on the nipple. Sasha flicks again. His body jerks but he does not make a sound, does not move his arm.

'I like your courage, your determination,' she says as she licks and lightly bites his burnt nipple. She raises her head and looks into his eyes. She is smiling but she isn't satisfied. She licks his lips, bites them, and then kisses them. A soft lingering kiss. She holds him by his waist, presses him against her pelvis and caresses his right nipple with her finger. He is getting hard again. She kneels down, holds his hardened dick and starts stroking it. Garun moves his pelvis forward. He wants more. His body and his needs are directing his actions now. He is being taken over by his desires. She continues to stroke him and just when he is about to cum, she stops. She looks up at him. 'Getting too excited, are you?' She gets up. Garun moves his pelvis forward again. He wants more. He does not want her to stop. And this is what gives her pleasure. She is in command, she is in control. It does not matter what he wants. He will get what she wants to give him.

'Why do you want to finish this off so soon?' she asks as she licks and bites his ear lightly. 'Tell me, what do you want next? Whips or kicks?'

'Whips.' Garun's lips quiver a little. He is sweating.

Sasha throws her head back and laughs. A sharp, vile, stinging laugh. 'You think you will always get what you choose? You think you are in charge?' Her expression has totally transformed. She frowns in anger. 'WRONG!' She yells and knees him hard in the balls. Garun's whole body tightens. She kicks him again and he shakes. She holds his arm. 'This is when things start to get rough.' She raises his right arm and straps it. After that comes an endless volley of kicks to his groin. His body stiffens and shakes, but he does not open his mouth, he does not make a sound. After more than twenty hard, cruel kicks Sasha takes a step back. Garun lets his body go loose. For the first time he opens his mouth, but not to utter a word or make a sound, only to breathe. He is panting hard. His body glistening with sweat. The fire in the fireplace has grown stronger. It is casting sharper shadows on the wall.

Sasha grabs Garun's balls again. This time, lightly, only to examine them. They are swollen, big and red. They are sore. She strokes his dick that has gone limp now. She plants several soft kisses on it and strokes it till it starts to harden and rise again.

It is a sight for her. Her face is glowing with satisfaction. Garun's emotions are lifting and falling just the way she wants, just the way she is controlling them. She lets his dick get a full erection again and it only takes two kicks to make it go limp. She looks down at his semi-erect dick and then at his face. She smiles. She takes a drop of sweat from his face on her finger and licks it. 'It's funny isn't it? Everything that oozes out of a man's body is salty. Be it his sweat, his blood, his piss, his shit or the cum he sends into a woman's body to carry life on. We are not like flowers. There is nothing sweet about us.'

She goes on.

'But you know something, I think there is a reason

for our "saltiness". Let's take a little break here. Let your willy relax a little. Let me tell you a little story someone told me once. It kind of explains the thing about this saltiness.' She looks at Garun who is hanging by his arms, exhausted. He looks back and nods. Sasha continues. 'They say that the greatest kind of high that can ever exist is what one gets from the oxygen in the air. All those drugs, those wines are worthless in comparison to the relief one gets from breathing oxygen.

'In the beginning, all life on earth existed under water. And all life followed the "machhli nyay", the rule of the fish, which stated one thing and one thing only – the big fish eats the small fish. All land was reserved for the gods to enjoy the greatest intoxicant of all. Air. The fish could only see them enjoying it through the watery, wavy vision from under the sea. One day, one brave fish approached the gods and pleaded to let them live on land. The gods refused at first but the fish was persistent. The gods finally agreed but on one condition – if the fish wanted to live on land, they had to forget the machhli nyay and follow the rules of the land. They would have to live in peace and harmony and always help the ones in need. The bigger, more powerful ones must never trouble or overpower the weak. The fish agreed and that's how life crawled on to the land. That's how life evolved on land.'

Sasha brings a glass of water from the table near the

fireplace to Garun's lips. He cranes his neck forward and eagerly drinks from it. Sasha goes on with her story, 'But time and again, humans forget their promise. They start following machhli nyay again. The rich start killing the poor. And that's when the gods intervene. This whole shit about power and money, this whole idea of capitalism, consumerism, it's not a sustainable model for society or the environment. But stupid humans, they will never understand. This world, it's all about money, it's all about appearances. And that's why it will end one day.'

She goes and places the empty glass back on the table. 'You want this money so badly. But remember, it is not going to do any good to you.' She walks to the wall and takes a whip off the hook.

'Enough of storytelling. Now let's get on with business.'

'It's funny, isn't it?' she says as she walks back to him. 'The human body and the human touch. A touch can arouse so many different kinds of feelings, so many different kinds of responses. The same touch on some parts of your body,' she says, running her hand up his abdomen to his chest, 'can make you feel so vital.' She licks his right nipple. She can see his dick growing hard again. 'But then, another touch,' she says as she walks around him and stands facing his back, 'can do the exact opposite of it.' She whips his back. Garun twists and turns as hard, sharp lashes rain on him. But this does not stop Sasha's relentless whipping. Only when she realizes that he has started to bleed does she stop. She goes to stands in front of Garun. His head hangs low. Sweat dripping from his face. The floor is shining with a thin film of sweat. He looks silently into her eyes for a while and then says, 'Is it over now?'

Sasha's frowns involuntarily. She clenches her teeth hard, gives one hard kick to his groin. 'Now it is.'

She unstraps his wrists. Shoulders drooping, panting heavily, he looks into Sasha's eyes. He sees fire, he sees burning anger. And then he does the unexpected. He holds her tight and kisses her. Sasha does not resist. He peels her light gown off her shoulders. Her light chiffon gown slumps on to the little pool of Garun's sweat beneath their feet. Losing its stiffness and volume, it slowly soaks in the sweat and and hugs the floor.

Sasha embraces Garun. She runs her hands on his bloody back. She can feel him hard against her pelvis. She wants him now.

Part 3

Lives so changed!

28

Garun

Now he can buy everything he has ever dreamed of

Whatever happened in the last few weeks must remain a secret. No one needs to know about it and no one *should* get to know about it. All that matters is that I have got a fuck load of money that is easily gonna last me a year, if not more. It was my worst nightmare come alive but it's all in the past now. I don't even wanna think about it. All I want to think about is what all I'll buy now. God! I could have never imagined I would get so much money in one single sweep. Seventy-five hundred thousand rupees is no joke, man! The market is busy today and I have shopped quite a bit. These Timberland shoes are just what I wanted but it's such a pain carrying all these bags to the parking.

'Hey Garun!' I hear someone call me. I turn around and see Tarush running up to me.

'Hey man, how are you?'

'I am good. How are you?' I put the bags down and shake his hand. This fucker is an important member of all the committees in college. I need to be nice to him.

'Good. Where have you been, man? Not seen you in college in weeks.'

'Yeah, I had to go somewhere.'

'Okay. Wanted to tell you that we have the college fest next week. I remember you telling me that you wanted to sing, poop star.' He winks.

Asshole.

'Oh yeah, good you remembered. Please put my name on the list. I have just finished writing a song. Would love to sing it.' All girls are suckers for love songs. I know it will catch Maya's attention. And writing a love song is the easiest thing to do. One just has to listen to a dozen good love songs over and over, let them run in your mind for a few days and then borrow the lyrics and replace the words. Synonyms rule!

'Done. And by the way, Maya will be there too. We are honouring her with a special award for her literary achievements. You will find her in the front row.' He winks again.

Great! This just makes my work a lot easier.

'Thanks,' I say.

'Okay, then. See you in college.'

'Cool.'

As he leaves, I turn around and put my new Tom Ford shades on and walk to my new red convertible Mercedes. As I drive out, everyone on the road gapes at me. They turn their stupid, worthless heads to look at me in amazement. I want to throw my head back and laugh as I accelerate. This is not even funny. Though my nuts are still a little sore, I have never felt better. I no longer have to worry about saving money for taxi rides back home, for the bills of all those seven-star hotels I took those bitches to. I am rich now. I just need to become famous. And this is the perfect time. It's time to take my plan to the next level. It's time to meet Maya again, and make her believe I love her more than anyone has ever loved her before. But all this money won't impress her. She is a hard bitch to crack. She is someone who shuns the power of money and the glorious principles of capitalism, someone who worships the beauty of art and culture. She is so stupid she does not even understand that it's only the rich and powerful who shape all art and culture. The art of any age is only meant to serve the likes and demands of the rich ruling class. If it wasn't for them, there would have never been any art in this world. History is testimony to that, whether it's the classic art of the Greeks and the Romans, or the sophisticated Renaissance music and paintings in Europe. It's only the rich who need and can appreciate art. The poor are too busy earning bread for their hungry, grumbling stomachs. They never give a shit about art. They only feed on food, and if anything at all, they feed on love. And love is what Maya needs to believe I am feeding her.

~

I wanted to take Maya for a drive in my new Mercedes but decided against it. I know she is terribly prejudiced against the rich. I met her in college and brought her here in an auto. Such low-class shit. We are at the Mehrauli Archaeological Park. I wanted to take her to one of Delhi's offbeat places. She is clearly not a mall person. And taking her to Dilli Haat or Qutub Minar would not have worked because they are always overcrowded. This was the best I could think of – the lonely and expansive park right next to Qutub Minar. It's a bright, sunny day. We sweat a little when we walk but when we sit down in the shade the cool wind is quite comforting. We are sitting under a huge, old neem tree. Just sitting there, not talking, not doing anything. I want her to get comfortable first. I didn't force her to come here. In fact she asked me why I hadn't been coming to college. She is interested but she has to ask the first question, she has to break the ice. She plays with the grass on the ground, plucks a blade off and smiles at it as if it's some sort of a trophy.

'Do you remember the old TV serial version of the Ramayana?' She finally speaks up.

'Not really. It was too slow for me to follow. I tried to watch it on YouTube but could not go beyond a couple of episodes. Looked quite dated too.'

She has got that stupid smile still plastered on her face. 'When Ravan abducted Sita, he kept her with some of his female demon guards in the grand palace garden.'

God. What shit is she gonna say to me now? That TV show was so boring.

'Sita was devoted to her husband, Rama, and warned Ravana not to lay a finger on her. She set her boundary by holding up a long blade of grass, telling him that he could talk to her but never come close. That blade of grass was her shield of protection.'

'Wow! Ravana must have been quite the gentleman.'

'Can't really deny that.' She smiles.

'But you don't need to worry about the whole "don't lay your finger on me" thing here. I have no intention of putting you through any trouble here.' I ease her with a smile. She smiles back at me.

It's time to give her the present I got for her. All girls like gifts, there are simply no exceptions. And it's good that she is not a sucker for gold and jewellery. I didn't want to waste my money on someone as stupid as her. I pull out a small box from my pocket and place it in front of her. After a few seconds of silence she asks, 'What is this?'

'Open it.' I tell her.

She opens it, moving her gaze between the box and me, confused. Her eyes widen when she sees what is in the box.

'Garun, I can't take this.'

'But . . . it's for you. What do you mean . . . you can't take it?'

'It's expensive, Garun. I can't take it.'

'No, no, it's not expensive. It's just packed to look expensive. It's cheap metal with gold plating on it,' I explain.

Still uncertain, she takes the flower-shaped locket in her hands. It's pretty. She can't deny that. It's shaped in the form of a delicate daisy, the kind that grows wild in the mountains. The petals are slender and thin and the central disc embedded with little red gems.

'No, I can't take this. Does not matter if it's expensive or not.'

She is weirder than I thought. 'But why?' I question.

'I can't really answer that but it's just that . . . I don't accept gifts,' she replies hesitantly.

'. . . But why?'

'I have my reasons. It . . . reminds me of someone.'

She tries to hand the box back. I do not take it from her. Then she puts it on the ground in front of me. An awkward silence prevails for a while. Finally she says, 'I don't really know anything about you. Tell me something about yourself.'

'Right now . . . something about *myself* would be that I am heartbroken because I got a very pretty gift for a beautiful girl I like and she refused to accept it.'

'Who all are there in your family?' she smiles and asks.

'Mom and Dad. I am their only child.'

'Where do you stay?'

'Gurugram.'

She wants to ask more but finds it awkward. I think I should tell her the story I have made up instead of waiting for her to ask more questions.

'I don't live with my parents actually,' I begin.

She looks at me. She wants to know more.

'My parents separated when I was a kid. Must have been around nine or ten years old. Thinking back, neither of them was really at fault. Dad got a really cool job in the US and Mom did not want to leave India. They slipped away from each other over the years. Mom runs an NGO called Arth. They work with women in remote villages across India. She never really had time to take care of me due to all the travelling. I have lived with my grandparents for most of my life. But now that

I am eighteen I am free to spend time with either of my parents as and when I like. My father bought me an apartment in Gurugram. That is where I stay now.'

'Where are your grandparents?'

'They live in Ambala.'

I given her a questioning smile. 'You never asked me where I was last week. Why I was not coming to college.'

'Why were you not coming to college?'

'My nani was not well.' I look down at the grass, making sure my eyes go misty as I speak.

'I am sorry. But what happened?' She is concerned.

'She had a bad case of food poisoning that developed into pneumonia because some water entered her lungs.' I have her full attention now.

'Is she okay now?'

'Yes, she is fine. Otherwise I would not have been here.' I smile at her.

'You should take care of them.'

'Thank you for your concern. Whatever I am today, wherever I have reached, it's only because of my nana and nani. I don't think I love anyone in this whole world as much as I love them. And it's more than my duty to take care of them in their old age. If they hadn't looked after me when I was a kid, I would have just ended up a useless street kid.'

I smile, pretending I am remembering my childhood. 'You know, when I was a kid, I never liked drinking milk. Initially I used to make her run after me, round and round the whole courtyard. One day she told me I could learn to fly if I drank milk.'

Maya smiled. 'Then? Did you believe her? Did you drink the milk?'

'Maya, I was a kid, not stupid. Of course I did not believe her. I knew if I wanted to fly all I needed was an Iron Man suit.'

She laughs. 'Then? Did your nani give up?'

'Oh no! She never gives up. She is a tough woman. She figured out that I loved ice cream. So she started putting ice cream in my milk. I started drinking it.'

'It's rare to see someone so attached to one's family these days.' She seems amused by my story. But the moment is quickly followed by another awkward silence.

'Did I tell you I have written a novel?' I try to keep the conversation going.

'No.' She shakes her head and frowns.

'Well, I have written a novel.'

'Published?'

'Of course.' God! Is she retarded? Why would I tell her I have written a novel if it was not published? 'In fact, I just got my royalty cheque for the quarter. That's how I could afford the present I got you.'

'I appreciate that you bought it with your own hard-earned money,' she says.

'So?' I nudge her.

'So?' She is still frowning.

'Are you gonna accept it now?'

She just looks back at me and smiles. She does not pick up the box.

29

Sasha
Her insatiable thirst

Sasha is back home after torturing and fucking Garun for a week. The remaining sessions were no different from the first. Just that she notched down the whipping a little. Garun had endured her sessions unlike any man she had thrashed before. He did not scream. Not even once did he beg her to let him cum. Is that why she is still thinking about him, two weeks after returning home? Her rule was to throw the money on the man's face after she was done with him and tell him to go away and never show her his face again. But somehow she had not said that to Garun. On the contrary, she had sent him home in her favourite black Porsche, chauffeur driven.

She has been contemplating this for a while. What's the harm in contacting him again? He wants money, she wants his body, it's fair trade.

She opens her laptop and sends him a message:

I want to meet you again. And just like our first meeting, no fucking, no touching, no stroking.

In less than thirty seconds the reply flashes in front of her.

When? And where?

She smiles and types her reply.

I will let you know soon.

30

Garun

To impress the girl

There is a flood of colourful lights beaming and dancing behind me. A firm, bright spotlight is fixed on me. There is a sea of people gathered in front of the stage. I spot Maya. She is standing in a corner, arms folded across her chest, her hair loose, framing her face on which she is wearing thick-rimmed glasses. I close my eyes, take a deep breath and start with the alaap of my song.

Beyond a sea of memories, ashes and dust,
my love lives.
Wandering in her loneliness, she turns the dust beneath
her feet into roses and daisies.

I open my eyes and look at Maya. She is listening. Her eyes are on me. I smile, close my eyes again and sing on.

On the other end of this sea, I shiver, I quiver with the cruel pain of separation.
The thought of the cool oasis of your lips, the desire of the touch of your skin keeps me alive.
Brighter than the sun in the sky is my love for you.
Stronger than the mountains, high and wide, is my love for you.
No power, no force can keep us apart. No God, no soul can be so cruel.
One day I will grow wings out of my love for you,
stronger than the swiftest bird I will fly across the seas
and fly you away to the beautiful land of pure love.

I finish the song and open my eyes. The crowd is going crazy. They loved it. I am, and have always been, a star. My eyes quickly scan the crowd to find Maya. She is gone.

~

I unsling the guitar from my shoulder, bow to the crowd, and quickly run off the stage. My eyes dart around to find someone I know when I feel a hand on my shoulder.

'Bro! That was brilliant! You are no poop star, man! You are a *rock star*!' I turn around to see Tarush. He has a high-tech headphone on with a tiny mic lining his jaw into which he suddenly starts speaking. 'No, no! Keep them off the stage, there's time before they perform. We have another performer before them! No!' He looks at me again and says, 'I've got to go, man, or they are gonna mess up the whole event.' He shakes my hand. 'Well done, that was really good.' He gives me a hug and is about to run away when I say, 'Wait! Did you see Maya anywhere?'

'She left, man,' he says hastily as he starts to walk away. 'Said she had some urgent shit to take care of at home. Won't be able to attend the award ceremony we have planned for her. Got to go. See you later.' He runs away.

What the hell happened? Why did she leave in the middle of the evening? Did this whole thing backfire? Instead of impressing her, did I offend her? Fuck!

31

Maya

Falling for someone . . . else

He sang for me today. He sang for me in front of the whole college. He looked at me once and I knew he had written the song for me. It was beautiful. It reminded me of one of my favourite songs by Faiz Ahmad Faiz. Garun's writing is that strong. I wish I had recorded the song as he sang it on stage. I wish I had made a video. It's a pleasant memory. It makes me smile.

My phone buzzes to life. It's a message from Garun. A video. He has sent me a video of his performance.

Arun is here with me. Until a few weeks ago he would visit me and go back. Now he is with me all the time. It's like we are living together.

'Arun, I just got the video.'

Arun turns around to look at me.

'See.' I sit down next to him and play the video. He listens to the song and smiles.

'Looks like he likes you,' he says. He seems happy.

Suddenly my heart feels heavy. Garun may or may not like me, how does that make any difference? I love Arun. And I don't want anyone else in my life. I am happy with him. 'What do you mean?' I frown.

'Looks like he likes you,' Arun repeats. 'Looks like he would care for you as much as I would.

I am scared. I sit there, frozen.

'If you let someone else into your life, Maya, it won't mean that you would lose me. I will always be there. I am a part of your life. Nothing can take me away from you. I am a part of your mind, your heart and your soul. But that does not mean you do not need anyone else to fill some other parts of your life.'

I look back at him blankly. I don't understand him. I don't want to understand him.

'But I want things to be the way they used to be. I want you back in my life . . . you were there with me . . . Don't *you* want me back in your life as we were?' I ask Arun.

Arun looks at me affectionately and says, 'I have enough memories with you to keep me happy till eternity. I don't need more.'

He lets this sink in and continues. 'I only want what is best for you, Maya. You must trust me.'

We look into each other's eyes. His eyes are my whole universe. It's like I am diving into a vast, infinite space. The stars, the moons, the suns, the galaxies, lights and shades of all the colours of love. I pass them by. I fly and float around them, feeling weightless, feeling more alive than I ever have. There is infinite love, infinite peace here. And I exist here. I exist in those eyes. I want to live in them forever. This is the true reason for my being. He is the true reason for my whole being. And he is asking me to make someone else a part of my life. The one I love wants me to love someone else. They say love always brings you to the right path. Arun is asking me to go with Garun. It must be the right thing to do.

32

Garun

His final move

'You liked the song?' She nods with a faraway look in her eyes directed towards the sky. I knew it. The song was sucked out of her all-time favourite, how could she not like it?

'It was a sensitive song,' she says, still lost, like a madwoman.

Then I notice something dreamy, romantic in Maya's eyes. We sit in silence for a while. I am sure Maya is imagining it to be the kind of silence they describe in those stupid romance novels – 'when-mouths-shut-and-their-hearts-talked kind of thing'. I can see that glow on her face they talk about. The shy hesitance to look into my eyes because she knows I can see her love for me in them.

'I read your novel,' she says.

'Really? Don't tell me!'

She nods again. That same light nod with the same dazed eyes. 'It was nice.'

'No way! Come on. It is a terrible novel.' I have to pretend. She has to buy that I'm a humble person.

'Seriously. It was nice. Very honest and innocent.'

'No way . . . But thank you. This coming from you means a lot. A hell of a lot.'

When she doesn't respond I add, 'I mean, you are an award-winning author, man. You are . . . you are really a great author.' I look down, feigning embarrassment.

'You think winning an award makes one a great author?' she asks.

'Of course it does. I mean . . . an award is testimony to one's talent.'

'Don't you think there are a lot of books being written,' she continues, 'and so many of them go unnoticed, unacknowledged. And so many of them are better, greater than the ones that get noticed.' She is talking to me but still seems to be lost in some strange world. At times I feel she is half crazy. But I don't care. In fact, if she is crazy, it would only make me feel less guilty for what I plan to do to her.

'Yes, all that. But that does not mean your book is any

less great than the other books. I mean . . . when I read that book . . . I cried. And trust me, I am not someone who cries easily. I am a tough kid.' I thump my chest with my fist as I puff it out.

She is still avoiding eye contact but now she has a faint smile on her lips.

'What are you writing these days?' I ask her.

'Nothing.' Her reply is instant, she does not even pause to think.

'What? But why?'

She shrugs.

'But Maya, you have so many fans out there. They love your book. They love *you*! They want more stories from you. Write for them, if not for anyone else. Your first book was such a phenomenal success.'

Silence.

'No, seriously. You should write.' I nudge her more. I have to push her to write again. I need reasons for her to spend more time with me alone. I need to give her more reasons to trust me.

She shakes her head. 'Seriously, I can't.' She finally looks at me. 'I am not really a writer. I can't imagine or make up stories. The book I wrote was something I had experienced, something I had lived. Those were my feelings that I wanted to share with people; people who might have gone through the same thing and were shattered; people who had lost the courage to live on.

Or for those who knew such people and wanted to help them. I don't have another story to share. I . . . I can't feel other people's feelings that well. I am not as . . . empathetic as one needs to be to be a writer. Most of the time I can barely step out of my own mind, my own thoughts. Making up stories and understanding other characters' feelings is a far cry.' She lets out a little laugh.

'You know what I think, Maya,' I say, 'once a writer always a writer. And come on. Don't you find writing addictive? I mean for me writing is the best kind of drug. It gives me the kind of high that no other drug can. Ever since my first book, I don't feel . . . complete if I don't write.' I am making things up on the go. I have to convince her by any means.

She looks at me, confused.

'Okay, reading your book I felt that you must be maintaining a diary, a journal.'

She nods. She still has that confused frown.

'So you just need to pick up clues from that. All of us, we live a story each day, each week, each month. You have it all there. We just need to change it a bit, camouflage it a little and we would have a novel.'

Her eyes are fixed on me. She is listening.

'I have been thinking about it for a long time now, Maya. Let's write a book together. Your writing is magical. If you find it difficult to think of a story, I can help you with it.'

I know I have her where I wanted.

'Maya, it really kills me to see you so sad and silent all the time. Seeing you like this . . . it kills me! I want you to take up something that puts your mind to something that would pull you out of this constant distress you are always in.'

Her eyes are still on me.

'I love you, Maya, and I want you to be happy, so that I can be happy again.'

33

Sasha

Any price to get him

She wanted to meet him in seclusion. She had decided to call him to Tughlaqabad fort. He is already there when she reaches. It is noon and the place is as deserted as it could be. Sasha had always found this fort mysterious. It had so many things present there in spite of not being present there. Time had eroded and scooped away a major part of it. But what was left was enough to tell the tales of what it had been through.

Garun is sitting on a pyre of stones which might have been a wall, or a pillar. Sasha goes and sits down next to him.

After a long awkward silence, Sasha says, 'Aren't you surprised I called to meet again?'

'Not really. I know I am quite irresistible. Women fall in love with me all the time,' he says cockily.

Sasha throws her head back and laughs. 'Oh please, don't get this wrong. I am not in love with you. Love is an emotion I am completely incapable of. I just want your body again, nothing else.'

Garun fixes his gaze on her meaningfully, as if to say that he knows her inside out, he knows she is lying.

'It's always foolish to think you know everything. You really don't know anything, Garun,' she says. 'You may think I am crazy, you may think I am mad, I am out of control and I belong to a mental asylum. But I'll tell you that's not true. I am totally aware of my passions and my behaviour. The human mind works very simply, Garun, the better ones among us want to help those who are weak, who are in despair, distress, who are in pain. We feel a strong affection for them, a boundless adoration for them, we love them more. This is exactly how I function. I would hit you, kick you. I would crush your balls, I would whip your naked body, I would make you weak. I would make your knees buckle. You would beg for mercy with your eyes, you would break, fall weak, give up due to the pain. And that's when I would feel a strong rush of affection for you. I would want to kiss you, fuck you, want you in me. Some may say that my subordinate passion has become predominant and I need treatment. I would only say that they know shit about what I feel.'

She pauses and looks at Garun who is listening to her silently. 'These are the dark parts of the human mind, Garun. People say they understand them, but they understand nothing.'

Then she gives him her proposition.

'You come with me for another week. This time I will pay you a lot more than last time. One crore.'

Without hesitation, without a single thought or doubt, Garun says, 'No.'

A long silence follows. Sasha was not expecting this.

'Take your time. Think it over. I am in no rush for an answer.'

'I just gave you my answer. It's not gonna change.'

Sasha does not utter a word but her eyes are on Garun.

'You are not the only way for me to make money,' Garun says. 'I got what I wanted out of you and I don't want to have anything more to do with you.'

This was certainly not how she had imagined things would go.

'What do you think, Sasha? You got all naked in front of me, you showed me all your paintings, all your scars, and that that would make me fall in love with you? Oh come on. Grow up. You are a middle-aged woman. No matter how much money you spend to look young, how many surgeries you undergo, you are never gonna be young again.'

'I will pay you double . . . one and a half million.'

Garun looks at her with rage burning in his eyes. Without raising his voice, he says, 'Listen, you slut. I said no. Go find someone else to treat your menopausal, midlife crisis.'

Sasha hears him out wordlessly but inside, her mind has never yelled and screamed harder – like an animal, wild and out of control. A smile creeps on her face. Without raising her voice, in a tone that betrays nothing of her internal turmoil, she says, 'You are going to pay for this, you bastard. You will pay a very heavy price for this. And I hope when that happens, when you are more miserable than a dying leper, you know who did that to you, who made you pay that price.'

With that, Sasha gets up and leaves. On the way home in her chauffeur-driven car she makes a call. All she says is, 'I am sending you a picture. He is at Tughlaqabad fort right now. I want you to start following him this instant and inform me of his every move.'

She is heartbroken, wounded and angry. Her soul is screaming in pain.

They say everyone is entitled to one true love in their life, and she has found her love in the wrong person.

34

Garun

What is the worst thing a guy can do to a girl?

I am so close to the next story that I want to write that I can't even believe it. People love to read true stories and I am gonna give them one like no other. They will sob over the story. They will cry their eyes out. It will be the saddest love story ever. It will be the biggest bestseller. And I will be the biggest author ever. It's time now to worship me for my infinite genius. But all this is still a few days away. Tonight is the night I make my bull happy. With the new car and the expensive clothes and shoes, picking up girls has become so much easier. And these hotel people also know me well now. They don't even mind me bringing girls. Those smaller hotels were getting nosier by the day. Hungry dogs. They just want more money. The room where I have brought this bimbo is quite impressive. I can turn on the fan, the AC or the lights just by saying it out loud. And it has lights for all moods – romantic lights, active lights and day lights. The room has huge paintings that I am sure those snobbish 'arty-farty' kinds would worship and rave about. All I see is that most of them are of nude men and women, which creates a good ambience for us to get rocking. The girl is smoking the joint I just rolled for her. She is blowing circles of smoke like a fish breathing out bubbles under water. Smoking cigarettes is for losers. Joints are the real deal. They transport you to another world. They stretch time for you. That trance is unparalleled. Like every other girl I have fucked, I have not asked her name. Neither has she asked mine. She also looks dumber than any other girl I have had before.

'Let's play a game,' I say, smoking the joint in my hand.

'Ahan . . .' The girl nods.

'So we both ask each other a question,' I say, puffing out a perfectly neat ring of smoke, 'and with each answer the other strips off a piece of clothing.'

'Sounds exciting.'

'No shoes or socks. I don't want to waste time on those,' I say.

'Deal!'

We take off our shoes and socks and sit on the bed facing each other.

'How long would you last if you were stranded on an island?' I shoot.

'Not more than a minute.' She laughs. 'I would jump into the sea and start swimming towards civilization.'

'Nice,' I say as I lean forward and take off her top. I am pleased with what I see beneath it. Her breasts are firm. She is wearing a black bra with a flowery lace along its edge. I run my fingers down her body as she smiles and arches her back.

'What is the longest time of uninterrupted pleasure that you have been able to give a girl?' she asks, teasing me with her eyes.

'It lasted over twenty-five minutes once.' She does not even listen to my answer properly and starts to unbutton my jeans. I look at her, smile and stand up. She pulls down my jeans along with my boxers.

'Hey! That's cheating.'

She gives me a sly smile. 'All is fair in love and war,' she says. She is happy to see me in a state of semi-erection. I am getting harder looking at the half-naked girl in front of me. I want to grab her by her hair, smack her hard, rip all of her clothes off and tear her limbs off as I fuck her hard. I want to do to her what I do to those bloody pigeons that invade my house. I want to tear her skin and lick her blood off her skin. Soak my hands in her blood. I want to kill her as I fuck her and I want to keep fucking her as her lungs draw their last breaths. But I can't do that. Killing a person is not that easy. One has to really plan it well.

'What is the worst thing one can do to a girl?' I ask her as I take out a condom and keep it ready.

'The worst thing one can do to a girl,' she says as she starts to crawl towards me, 'is rape her.' She pounces on me and rips off my shirt. It doesn't take me more than a second to pull down her tight pants along with her panty. She is already wet and I am rock-hard. I pull on the condom and enter her as she throws her head back and moans. I pull her hair back in a tight grip and lick her neck. It's good that the worst thing a guy can do to a girl is rape her. Because that is not what I am gonna do to Maya. I am not that evil a person after all.

35

Sasha

Bones crunching, fountains of blood

If she sets her mind to something, nothing can stop her. Nothing can come in her way. From the moment Sasha had made that phone call, Sasha had been waiting like a restless child for information on Garun. Her hatred for him was consuming her. The hatred was almost like an organism – evil, unstoppable. Living inside her, eating away at her mind. Growing. People said such hatred was toxic and killed whoever harboured it. How wrong they were. This was her fuel, her power. This was what drove her, gave her strength. How could he say those things to her? Did he not know who she was? The mere thought of Garun made her blood boil. Blind with rage. There had to be something, some secret she could use to get total control over him. Absolute. No one had ever said no to her. No one had ever dared to.

She turned on her laptop to check her email. Her eyes lit up with satisfaction. It was the email she had been waiting for.

From: service@hakkamail.com
To: sasha1920@hakunamail.com
Subject: At your request

Dear Ma'am,

We have retrieved the following information about the subject.

(1) Garun is dating a girl from his college. She is suffering from clinical depression. Due to the drugs she has been prescribed, she hallucinates as well. Her name is Maya.

(2) Garun got an enormous amount of money recently. We are still in the process of figuring out where he got that money from.

(3) Garun's cruelty towards animals is not normal. We procured an old CCTV footage from his residence (kitchen camera) in which he is killing a pigeon. We are sending you the footage as an attachment with this mail. It was a high-definition camera. We were able to zoom in and crop.

Sasha downloaded the video and quickly wrote a reply.

From: sasha1920@hakunamail.com
To: service@hakkamail.com
Subject: Re: At your request

Thank you for the information. Please keep updating me with more.

PS: No need to find out where he got the money from.

It was time to watch the video. Sasha looked composed and peaceful but inside, she was jumping like a little kid who has just got a new, exciting toy. Dating a girl with mental health issues. Why? Abnormally cruel to animals. Why? With a new thrill bubbling inside her, she played the video.

There was no sound but Sasha could almost hear the bones of the pigeon breaking like dry twigs. The tiny fountain of blood that sprang from the point where the pigeon's leg was attached to its body just an instant ago. One twist of the neck. Then another. And another. The limp, lifeless neck hanging, swinging. Trashed in the bin. The counter wiped clean of all the blood. Garun washing his hands and walking away so casually, as if he had done something as normal and regular as waking up in the morning and dumping his shit into the pot. The ugliness. The gore.

Sasha sat in her chair, transfixed. Her mind was still processing what she had seen, trying to make sense of it. Why would someone do such a thing? She had her reasons for the pleasures she got out of beating men. Hitting them. Making them bleed. They were criminals. Cheating. Hurting their partners. Leaving them emotionally scarred for life. Even ruining some lives in the process. How many bright minds were lost just because someone broke their heart once? How many bright, promising women! Helpless. But even then she had never wanted to or tried to kill a man. Was it his immaturity or was he deranged? She knew about his lust for money. She had seen it in his eyes. Was that driving him mad? Making him so blind and insensitive to everything around him?

Sasha turned off her laptop but she was still not able to shake the horrifying and ugly images out of her head. People had called her heartless and cruel. Then why was this so disturbing for her? Cruel people enjoy watching cruel actions, don't they? Was she losing herself?

36

Maya

Should she cross the line?

'Garun let me drive his car today,' I say. 'I felt so free.'

Arun looks at me and smiles. 'He believes in you.'

I nod.

'I was hesitant when he first suggested I should drive. It had only been a few months but it felt like I had not driven for ages. I was a little scared. The memory of the crash surfaced as soon as I held the wheel. "What happened?" Garun asked. "You look like you saw a ghost." I just shook my head. Then he put his hand on my shoulder and looked deep into my eyes. "What happened?" he asked. There was concern in his voice. I shook my head again. "You can trust me," he said. I held back my tears. "Nothing really. It's just that I met with an accident some time back. The memory has not faded.

The fear is still fresh." He laughed. "That's it? Come on, Maya! People get into car accidents all the time. But as long as they don't die, no one gives up driving." I was not sure but he held my hand and said he would not let me get out of the car if I didn't drive. And that I could take as long as I wanted. He said I knew how much he loved my company. Then suddenly he said that it might be a nice idea if I did not drive. We could just sit there for a whole week. He said he would do anything to stay there with me in the car. He has a cute boyish charm about him.' I smile.

Arun is looking at me. He wants to know what happened next.

'He pulled out the keys and that's when I grabbed them and turned on the ignition.'

'So you drove a car today.' Arun smiles.

I nod. 'I could because he believes in me, he actually believes in me.'

'Do you like him?' Arun asks me after some time.

I am scared to say what I feel.

'I want you to be happy, Maya. I want you to fall in love again.'

'I don't know Arun . . . at one level I feel that by having feelings for Garun, I am cheating on you. We are entitled to only one true love in our life and you are my true love. I can never love anyone the way I loved you. We were to spend our life together the way everyone else does. At times I feel I found my true love in the wrong person. And the mere thought burns me, destroys me. How can you be the wrong person? You are the most . . . right person in my life ever. You are the rightest thing that ever happened to me. The very thought feels like a sin.'

'I would understand if you said that I was the only true love of your life. But you have to understand that you need someone in your life like everyone else. You said it yourself. And when life has brought that person to you and made him stand right in front of you, I think you should accept him.'

Arun is looking deep into my eyes. He is looking inside me. He *is* me.

'I don't know, Arun. I do like him but it's just that . . . I can never like him the way I liked you. No one can be as special as you were.'

'But that does not mean you can never be with anyone else again.'

Silence.

'You deserve companionship, Maya, why won't you accept it?'

Silence.

'Say something, Maya. Please say something.'

'I just did, Arun. I can't think about him the way I think about you.'

Arun lets out an exasperated sigh. 'That's because you have still not let go! You are still holding on too tight. I am your past, Maya. Garun is your future. And being with him will not diminish your feelings for me. You would not be cheating on me if you are with him.'

Silence.

'Maya, I want you to do something for me one last time. You say you still have me in your heart and you can't think beyond me. It is because you have still not strengthened your relationship with Garun as you should have.'

I want him to say more but he falls silent. The seconds that follow feel like years. And in those seconds I relive my whole life with Arun.

'What do you mean?' I finally break the silence.

'You need to take your relationship with Arun forward, Maya. You need to be more intimate with him. You need to be more intimate with him than you ever were with me. You have to be one with him. Only then will you be able to put our relationship behind you.'

Silence.

'You can't make things happen, Maya, especially those that are not meant to. You can't force us to be together forever.'

I want to refute him. I want to yell at him for what he has just said. I want to grab him by his collar and slap him hard. But I can't move. I am a block of ice, frozen so that I can only see things around it but can't touch them. I sit there mute. Helpless. Trapped. I have lost my voice.

37

Sasha

When she meets Maya

The black Mercedes is parked across the road outside the coffee shop where Maya and Garun sit next to the window like two crazy lovebirds. Maya's dark hair is a glowing shade of brown in the golden light of the setting sun. Her face glows too. She looks happy. They sit with their elbows on the table. Holding hands. The image of his hands flashes in Sasha's mind as she spies on him from her car. Garun's hands. Not too hard, not too soft. Not too heavy, not too light. The slight trace of veins popping out below the knuckles. Fingers, not sausage thick, not spaghetti thin, the kind of hands she desired all over her body. Why is she paying so much attention to Garun, after all? Putting everything aside and coming here to follow him like this, what sense does it make? She could have easily picked up another man to play with. Why is she here? What is making her do this? Is she getting obsessed with him?

Yes, she is getting obsessed with him. But it is not because of the appeal of an unattainable love, as many would think. It is because of the strong hate that has sprung in her heart for him.

They talk for a while, Maya and Garun. Then Garun holds Maya's face in his hands, kisses her on the forehead and leaves. Maya's eyes follow him as he steps into his car and drives away. She then pulls out a sketchbook from her bag and starts sketching.

Sasha steps out of her car and walks over to the cafe. Is she going to talk to Maya? Is that the purpose? She does not know. She just wants a closer look. She just wants to know her. Sasha pushes the door open and looks around the cafe. It is jam packed. No vacant table. She turns around and finds Maya sitting alone by the window. Lost in her own thoughts, drawing, soaking in the golden sunlight. The street is busy – fast cars, horns, people yelling. There is a lot of chatter and clutter inside as well. But none of that makes any difference to her. She is engrossed in her work, as if in a bubble.

Sasha walks over to her table.

'Excuse me.'

Maya looks up after making a few strokes with her charcoal pencil.

'Can I please share this table with you? There is no other place.'

Maya smiles and says, 'Sure,' and continues working on her sketch.

Sasha sits down, stealing a peep as frequently as she can while pretending to study the menu. Maya's sketch is unusual. Strong, bold lines and free strokes. An interesting mix of linear and curvilinear lines that evolved forms which are fantastic and unearthly. She wants to talk to her, just a friendly conversation over a cup of coffee. But what should she say? What could they talk about? Moreover, she is drawing – creating art. It would be rude to interrupt.

So she just sits there for a while. She has a thing for artists. Art was something, she believes, that this world could never have enough of. When she was Maya's age, she wanted to be an artist. Art makes us feel, art makes us see things we can never otherwise see, it gives us eyes, it makes us sensitive to things we have been insensitive to. Sitting there on that chair opposite Maya she is slowly slipping into memories of her own past. Sinking. Something starts to suffocate her. Has she lost her chance? When she was younger she had been so clear what she wanted from her life. Has she wasted it all? Has she wasted her whole life on this destructive rampage? Creating a positive change only in her own mind, in her imagination? The men she thinks she has taught a lesson to . . . did they ever really change? Or did they become worse? The discomfort rises inside her, becoming unbearable. She can't breathe. The air around her feelss heavy, thick, difficult to suck in, like honey, only poisonously bitter. She puts on her shades and leaves.

Maya seems to be a simple girl. What does Garun want from her? She knows that Garun is incapable of an emotion like love. He is incapable of thinking beyond himself. Is Maya blind to this? Can someone actually be so naive?

38

Sasha

Nausea!

There is blood on the sheets. The man is tied to the bed. Raw, coarse jute ropes strapping down his neck, torso, waist, thighs and ankles. He is screaming as hard as his lungs have the capacity to. Sasha strikes him across his face. 'Don't scream!' she yells. But the man screams even harder now.

Sasha takes out a knife, eight inches, runs it swiftly across his chest, nipple to nipple. Making sure it only pierces the skin, she carves a neat line on his body. The precision of a professional butcher. Blood starts oozing out instantly, forming a string of red beads on his chest. Sasha smiles. The man screams harder. Sasha traces the bleeding wound with her finger, licks the blood. The man is screaming so hard that the corners of his mouth start to split. The tear grows larger and reaches the base of his neck. His eyes grow bigger, like balloons rapidly filling with water. They grow milky. Completely white. And then suddenly they burst. Sasha stares into his eye sockets for a while and then digs her finger into one; it is filled with a creamy, gooey liquid. She licks it off her finger. Suddenly the man's body, which was struggling painfully a moment ago, goes still. Like a slab of ice. It turns hard. And within seconds it starts to shrink. Rapidly. Turns into a worm. A thin, long, man-sized worm. Sasha continues to stare as the thing turns to dust on the bed and then vanishes altogether.

Sasha is tossing and turning on her bed. Uneasy, uncomfortable. She does not jolt out of her sleep but it wears off slowly, like a cloud drifting away. She sits upright in bed. The dream has left her throat dry. She grasps the glass of water by the side of her bed and drinks it all in a gulp. She feels sick. Somehow the water does not taste right. It tastes like blood. It tastes like the creamy, gooey eye liquid she had just licked in her dream. Suddenly something starts rising inside her and fills her mouth. Before she even realizes, her puke is all over the bed. She is wide awake now. The vomit, the slime – which is the colour of her dinner –

is soaking the bed sheets. The nauseating smell hangs in the air. She is unable to make any sense of what has just happened. She was dreaming about something she loved and had enjoyed for years. Why did it turn into such a nightmare? Why did it shake her up so badly? Why did it make her nauseous?

39

Garun

Triumph of death 1

The spider is hungry. I have not fed it for days. I transfer two flies into its glass case, close the lid and sit down to watch. There is no greater amusement than watching an animal hunt. It is way better than *Game of Thrones*, *The Walking Dead* or any other shit on TV.

The spider has spun its web well in the glass case. The fly doesn't really have a chance. After a few seconds of crashing against the glass, it is trapped in the web during one of its pointless escape attempts. As soon as the fly is trapped, the spider comes out of hiding. This is the best part. Slowly the spider advances as the fly struggles to free itself, only facilitating the sticky web to strengthen its grip on it.

Well done, my little Spidey. Good job for the day. And it's not only your lucky day today. I am in luck too. Just like you had this fly trapped in your web, the one that you just ate, I have Maya perfectly ensnared too. Today all my dreams are gonna come true.

~

The Aravalli range runs along the border of Gurugram. I have grown up on stories of India's most wanted criminals staying or hiding here. That is why people stay away from it. That is why I am here today. I did not want anyone disturbing me.

I spread the spotless white cotton sheet on the ground and take out the nicely prepared picnic basket from the boot of the car. I have removed all the rocks, small and big, from the ground where I have spread the sheet. It's a rugged terrain. I look at the rocks scattered around. They are sharp, hard and strong just like me.

'Didn't I tell you this was the most peaceful place for us to work? Just listen to this silence. You can hear the thoughts in your mind echo.' I smile as I look at Maya and sit down next to her on the white sheet.

She nods.

'Great! So I'll tell you the story I have in mind. Let me know how you like it. Feel free to add or subtract anything you like.'

Maya nods again. She seems to be lost in the thoughts of another world.

'So there is this girl. Young, beautiful. Not only has she lost her parents in a terrible accident, she has also been kicked out of her school because she has no money to pay the fees. She suffers from acute clinical depression but she does not realize that herself. No one has time for her, all her friends and relatives are busy with their own lives. One day she decides to kill herself. She writes a suicide note and decides to hang herself from the ceiling fan. She has been unaware of the young boy, her neighbour, who has always been hopelessly in love with her. He has been spying on her from his window, with a pair of binoculars. The day he sees her hanging a noose from the fan, he rushes to her rescue and over time draws her out of her depression. This is the basic storyline, how do you like it?'

'It's good . . .' is all she utters.

'Great! I am so relieved to know that you like it. God, I was so nervous that you might hate it. Wow! You are such a great writer and you like my idea. I feel I am in seventh heaven!'

She smiles.

'Okay. So I think we should start the book with the suicide note. I think that will be a good hook for readers.' I look at her hopefully.

'You want me to write it?' She finally gets the hint after what feels like an eternity.

'Of course! The book must open with your words. It would bring us tremendous good luck.' I hand her the pen and the notebook that I have ready.

She takes them hesitantly and opens the first page of the notebook. She looks at the blank paper in front of her and then she looks at me. I nod, urging her to write.

The pen in her hand moves faster than I expected it to. It is as if she is writing something she already knew, or something she had prepared and knew each word by heart. In less than two minutes, she hands the notebook back to me. One full page in blue ink, not less than two hundred words. Before I can read what she has written, I hear her call my name.

I look at her and find her eyes fixed on me, unblinking. We are drowned in silence when she slowly leans towards me. She is confusing me. All this time she has been throwing it in my face that a relationship does not need to be physical to be strong and now she wants to kiss me and make it all physical? But how does that matter to me? I will give her what she wants.

She comes and lightly touches her lips to mine and looks into my eyes. I gaze into her eyes burning with passion. She kisses me again and I hug her. She hugs me back. I don't know what has got into her but there is no way I am holding myself back. I never say no to free sex.

~

We do it under the open sky. Our bodies sweat. She is furious when it comes to sex. She has things hidden deep inside her. I could never have imagined her to be so hot and fiery. We are way past our orgasms but she is still hugging me so tight that I can barely breathe.

Time is passing by. I can almost hear a clock ticking in my mind. Why should I delay my plan? I look around. There is not a single soul in sight. I can't even see any birds in the sky, just this empty rugged hillock and the city far below it. I sit up and slip to the edge of the sheet, right next to the scattered rocks on the ground. Maya looks up at me and smiles. Her eyes still look dreamy. I smile back at her as I tighten my grip around the biggest rock I can grab. She has no idea what is coming. She turns her gaze away and that is when I strike her first. Right on the base of her head – it has to work. After one strike she is unconscious. I turn around her limp, naked body to check. Perfecto – no movement and the pupils are dilated. Just as I am about to start smashing her face so that it is beyond recognition I see a flicker of movement in her hands. She starts to frown. Fucking hell! She is gaining consciousness. I cannot afford to have her scream. I quickly jump to the picnic basket and grab the two pieces of cloth I had put in it. I roll up one into a ball, shove it into her mouth and use the other to cover her mouth completely. Now she won't be able to make a peep no matter how hard she tries.

Her eyes are wide open with panic. She tries to get up and run but I grab her and bind her hands and feet. I grip her hair and pull her head back. 'Don't make this more difficult for yourself. I want it to be as painless as possible,' I hiss. She tries to wriggle out of my hold and scream but only faint, muffled sounds escape her. I pin her down by her shoulders as she twists and tries to crawl away. Why won't this bitch just lie down peacefully so that I can finish her off? She is infuriating. With the rock tightly gripped in my hand I smack her face. 'Shut up! Or I will make you suffer more,' I spit out. I give her another blow with the rock in my hand. Her face starts to bleed. One side of her face is bloody. I throw more blows on her face till it looks like red pulp. She has passed out because of the pain. I stand up and look at her listless, naked body lying at my feet. Scratching my chin I deliberate if I should give her some more. Maybe a few more blows would make it look more natural. I pick up the rock again and smash it on her ribs. A few times more and it looks perfect.

Her legs and her chest get the same treatment. She is covered in blood now. Perfect!

I unbind her hands and feet, remove the cloth from her face and her mouth and pull her to the edge of the cliff.

'Goodbye, my love. Your death is gonna be my gateway to fame and success,' I whisper. I grip her ankles and in one swift move send her flying off the cliff. I see her body crash against the rock before it finally lands on the ground with a thump. I always wanted to see someone fly. The pure joy of the spectacle brings a smile to my face. I pick up the white sheet that is all splattered with blood. I wipe my hands on it. I will need to burn it later.

The suicide note Maya had written is lying safe under a stone. This needs to remain here for the police. But I need a copy of it. I need to put it in the 'true story' of a tragedy-stricken girl who was never able to gather the shattered pieces of her broken heart, and ultimately decided to kill herself. The world is a sucker for tragedies and I'm gonna throw one at them and become the biggest author ever. I click a picture of the suicide note, put my clothes back on and sit in my lovely red car.

40

Garun

Triumph of death 2

Garun puts on loud music in his car. So loud that it shuts out the world around him. He is bobbing his head to the beats and presses the accelerator even harder. He is on top of the world today. His dreams have come true. He has got the perfect story – a guaranteed bestseller, an absolute tear-jerker. He is completely lost in his thoughts. He is almost living his success already, oblivious to the realities around him. Blind to the speeding bus behind him trying to outrun the car it has just scraped. He does not notice the truck ahead of him that has long steel bars hanging out of the back. The rage that rises inside him when the bus rams into his car giving it a powerful thrust doesn't even register properly because that very thrust sends his car hurtling forward, right into the steel bars. The windshield smashes. In less than a second, the bars have pierced his body, pinning it to his seat, like a fly pinned on an insect collector's board. One of the bars goes in through his eye and out from the back of his skull, spilling a part of his brain out. One bar goes in through the centre of his forehead sending a part of his brain gushing out of his nose like snot. One bar goes through his mouth open in a scream. But before the scream can come out, the bar goes in and emerges from the back of his neck, detaching his skull from the rest of his body, snapping his spinal cord. Garun's death is considerably painless and merciful compared to the way he had tried to kill Maya. Sharp sprays of blood from different parts of his body jet out and colour the interiors of the car red. Splashes of blood hit the windscreen. He does not experience the pain for more than a few seconds. His life and all his dreams of fame and success die instantly. How fragile is human life. How futile are human dreams and desires. The time it took him to die was so short that it was even hard to measure.

As the three vehicles come to a halt, blood oozes out of the many punctures from Garun's body, embedded in the seat of his expensive red Mercedes. Not even a single thought of Sasha comes to his mind before his brain dies and his heart stops pumping his hot blood through his veins.

It is an accident that people will talk about for some time. It is an accident that people who saw it will remember for the rest of their lives. 'His body is completely crushed. His face is not even recognizable any more,' someone says from the crowd that has gathered around him. 'May God never give such a death to anyone,' says another. 'We have to call the police,' comes a suggestion. 'Yes, the culprit must be punished. We have caught the bus driver,' another says. The bus driver can be seen at a distance. He had jumped off the bus and was trying to escape but was intercepted. His hands and feet are tied up now. Brutal blows and kicks are raining on him. It is quite possible that the mob will kill him before the police arrive. At times people find it to be their duty to bring justice for some crimes. Or is it that there is a higher power at play and the people are simply instruments?

41

Maya

Her fate, her destiny

Maya tries to open her eyes but the blinding light makes her shut them back. She slowly opens them again. She gradually comes to her senses and that's when the pain sets in, so excruciating she can't even scream. She feels nauseous. She pukes and collapses. But she has to live, she will not give up. She gathers all her courage and power and raises her head again. Her sight is faint and blurry, almost like a dreamscape, like a mirage. There is no one around. Not even Arun. He had always followed her like a shadow but now he is gone. And something inside her tells her that she will never see Garun again either. The power of her will is strong and she wishes him to die a cruel death. She is on her own now. She sees a road at a distance. She drags herself out of the bushes. She sees an ambulance next to a big black car and a woman standing next to it who comes running to her as soon as she spots her. She has never seen that woman before. Or has she? But she has to reach out to her, she has to drag herself to life. She has the power and she must live on. Not only because she is meant to, but because she wants to.

The woman comes and holds her. Her touch is comforting. 'I don . . . wa . . . die . . .' Maya struggles to speak, 'I wan . . . to . . . live . . .'

The woman looks at her. Eyes firm. 'You will,' she informs her. 'You will.'

Maya wants to get up and stand on her own feet but she doesn't have the energy to even hold her head up. She collapses.

42

Sasha

Turn, turn, turn

A black Mercedes trailed the ambulance that was taking Maya to the hospital. Speeding. Inside sat an anxious Sasha. Heart sinking. This girl must not die! She must be saved! She closes her eyes and rests her head on the head rest. Images of the girl's wounded body flash in her mind. Her battered face. Bloody. This one image followed by the face of a man she had once scratched with her bare, sharp nails. The image of the girl's shredded breasts . . . the image of the man's chest she had whipped bloody . . . that trail of blood on his torso . . . the girl's belly – bloody, pulp . . . the belly of the man she had once run her knife across, slicing skin, oozing blood . . . the girl's feet – skin scraped off, raw, covered in blood and filth

. . . the man's ankles tied tight with ropes, scratched raw, blood dripping into a tiny pool by the leg of the bed. Her head started to spin. Suffocation. Nausea.

'Stop the car!' she barks.

The driver hits the brakes.

She flings the car door open and throws up. One big, loud bout. Then another. And another. The driver hands her a bottle of water. She drinks, sits in the car, throws herself back against the seat, shuts her eyes tight. And then, all of a sudden, she sobs. Uncontrollably. It's an involuntary reaction. She clenches her teeth as she cries. She wipes her tears, rubs her eyes hard like a little kid. She sobs. After a long time, her tears slowly dry off. She can feel her heartbeat stabilizing. Things are okay now. Things are fine. That girl will be fine. She has to be. Sasha will make sure. She will get her the best treatment. She can't die. She just knows she can't. She will save her even if it demands everything she has got. All this while, though, there is a question lingering at the back of her mind: will she still torture men the way she used to?

But then, she sort of already knows the answer to that.

'The soul lives a life in the shadows . . . it is no longer able to see what it must see . . . It can no longer repose within its own being because it is constantly drawn to the external things . . . inferior and darker . . . sensible and bright . . . it has blended with many circumstances . . .'

Plotinus, *The Enneads*

A Note on the Author

Rahul Saini is the bestselling author of many novels, including *Those Small Lil Things: In Life and Love* and *Paperback Dreams*.

AN EXTENSIVE LIBRARY

Including fresh, new, original Juggernaut books from the likes of Sunny Leone, Praveen Swami, Husain Haqqani, Umera Ahmed, Rujuta Diwekar and lots more. Plus, books from partner publishers and loads of free classics. Whichever genre you like, there's a book waiting for you.

CRUCIBLES OF SIN
HITESHA
Can a Geek ever find Love?
Finding Juliet
Toffee
Mary Shelley
Frankenstein
A FAROOQ RESHI INVESTIGATION
COLD FLAKE
PRAVEEN SWAMI
A Psychiatrist's Guide To Heartbreak
How to Heal Your Broken Heart
DR SHYAM BHAT
MOIN and THE MONSTER
BY ANUSHKA RAVISHANKAR
stories of women from the ganglands
S. Hussain Zaidi
with Jane Borges
Foreword by Vishal Bharadwaj
UMERA AHMED
Nowhere Girl
A Story of Love & Forgiveness
THE BEHEADING
This Is How He Will Bless Her
ABHEEK BARUA
THE Peshwa
The Lion and the Stallion
THE INVISIBLE WOMAN
SAURBH KATYAL
ANGRY BIRDS FAN? READ THE BOOK!
ANGRY BIRDS TOONS
TOONS TALES
ARCHANA SABOO
ADIKOOL
in
#AfricanAdventures
i am not a bimbette
Tarana Khan
She hates me, He loves me not but...
DON'T FALL IN LOVE
Vandana Shankar
KHUSHWANT SINGH
WE INDIANS

We're changing the reading experience from passive to active.

juggernaut.in

Ask authors questions

Get all your answers from the horse's mouth. Juggernaut authors actually reply to every question they can.

Rate and review

Let everyone know of your favourite reads or critique the finer points of a book – you will be heard in a community of like-minded readers.

Gift books to friends

For a book-lover, there's no nicer gift than a book personally picked. You can even do it anonymously if you like.

Enjoy new book formats

Discover serials released in parts over time, picture books including comics, and story-bundles at discounted rates. And coming soon, audiobooks.

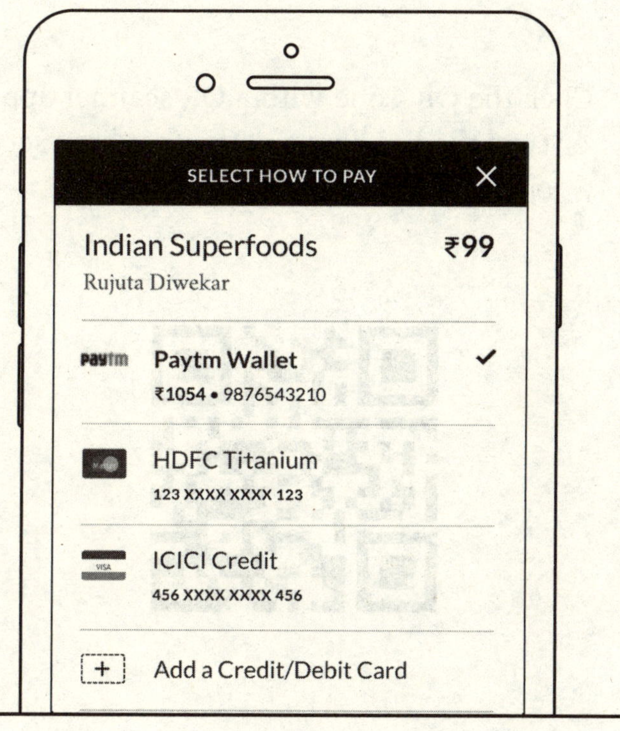

Paytm Wallet, Cards & Apple Payments

On Android, just add a Paytm Wallet once and buy any book with one tap. On iOS, pay with one tap with your iTunes-linked debit/credit card.

Click the QR Code with a QR scanner app
or type the link into the Internet browser
on your phone to download the app.